THE LAST BOOKS
OF
H.G. WELLS

The Last Books
of
H.G. Wells

The Happy Turning
&
Mind at the
End of its Tether

Book and cover design by Georgia Dent
Picture by Ronald Procter: H.G. Wells shakes fist at the 'vast lumping Sycamore' of THE HAPPY TURNING, Chapter 8

Provenance Editions
Volume 4

Library of Congress Cataloging-in-Publication Data

Wells, H. G. (Herbert George), 1866-1946.
  The last books of H.G. Wells / H.G. Wells ; new forwords by Colin Wilson and Rudy Rucker. -- Monkfish ed.
     p. cm.
  ISBN 0-9766843-1-4 (alk. paper)
  I. Wells, H. G. (Herbert George), 1866-1946. Happy turning. II. Wells, H. G. (Herbert George), 1866-1946. Mind at the end of its tether. III. Title.
PR5774.H3 2006
823'.912--dc22

                          2006031624

Bulk purchase discounts for educational or promotional purposes are available.

First printing

10 9 8 7 6 5 4 3 2 1

Provenance Editions are published by:
Monkfish Book Publishing Company
27 Lamoree Road
Rhinebeck, New York 12572
www.monkfishpublishing.com

CONTENTS

Introduction to THE HAPPY TURNING by Colin Wilson.................... vii

THE HAPPY TURNING.. 3

Foreword to MIND AT THE END OF ITS TETHER by Rudy Rucker..... 37

Preface by H.G. Wells... 40

MIND AT THE END OF ITS TETHER...................................... 42

About the Contributors... 65

THE HAPPY TURNING, the last but one of H. G. Wells's books, was written at the end of his life, when he was suffering from his final illness, the cancer of the liver that would kill him. Yet, unlike his last book, MIND AT THE END OF ITS TETHER, it is not a pessimistic work. On the contrary, it captures a mood of happy reminiscence when, suddenly freed from the sense of oppression brought about by the war, he experiences an odd sense of relaxation and happiness, as his unconscious mind decides to rescue him by sending interesting dreams.

Wells describes how he takes a daily walk from his home near Regent's Park down to his club in Mayfair, and how, in his dreams, he has begun to find a turning that he has never seen before. He wanders in a pleasant dream world where anything can happen, including conversations with Jesus, who has harsh things to say about St Paul for inventing the religion that Shaw would label 'Crosstianity'.

I was immediately reminded of an earlier story, written about 1910, called 'The Door in the Wall', which has always been a favourite of mine.

It is told to the narrator by a politician named Wallace, a member of the cabinet. He tells how, as a child of five, he was wandering down a street near his home in West Kensington when he saw a white wall, and a green door that stood open. And on the other side there was a magical garden, which even contained tame panthers who rubbed against him like friendly cats. He feels a 'keen sense of homecoming', and is met by a tall kind girl, who takes him by the hand. He meets other children and plays games, and a dreamy woman who shows him a book about himself. Then he finds himself back in the long grey street and back in a grey world.

He saw it again as a schoolboy, then passed it in a cab on his way to go up to Oxford, and again as a young man on his way to see his ladylove. He is always in a hurry and passes it. And now, he tells the narrator, he has seen it three times in a year. And has passed it each time, for political life holds out the prospect of success which he feels to be more important than that door 'into peace and delight'. But next time, he tells the narrator, he will go through it.

He is found dead at the bottom of a deep shaft made by workmen. It has been surrounded by a fence with a door in it, which has accidentally been left open.

That story clearly connects Wells with the romantics of the 1890s, that 'tragic generation' Yeats wrote about, who rejected the real world as too coarse and stupid for the sensitive soul. But by the time he wrote it, Wells was a highly successful writer, the author not only of the early scientific romances, but of novels like THE HISTORY OF MR POLLY and TONO BUNGAY. At the age of 45, he may have felt a twinge of suspicion that he has also 'sold out' to success.

When my daughter Sally was about 5, we took her to see THE WIZARD OF OZ. And as we came out of the cinema she said with sudden conviction 'I wish there was a land over the rainbow'. And suddenly I experienced that immense sadness of grasping how much children wish they didn't have to grow up into this practical world that they don't really like.

Was Wells, that remarkable prophet of things to come, really a romantic MANQUÉ? The other day, when preparing to write this Introduction, I selected half a dozen biographies of him off my shelf, and spent an afternoon browsing through them. And I realised with sudden clarity something that I had only half-grasped so far. For a man of genius — which he certainly was — Wells was curiously unsure of himself. Compare him, for example, with Joyce, and you see that he lacked a clear self-image. Stephen Dedalus has no doubt that he will be a writer of major importance. But in Wells's self-portraits - in the cockney cyclist Hoopdriver in THE WHEELS OF CHANCE, who falls in love with a pretty middle-class runaway, or Kipps, who settles for the working-class Ann Pornick, or Mr Polly, who daydreams romantically of a pretty girl in a private school who betrays him by bringing her school friends to listen-in to his romantic declarations — we always feel that he holds a low opinion of himself. The endless love affairs for which he became notorious may be seen as attempts to reassure himself, and improve his self-image. By the time he came to write THE HAPPY TURNING in 1943, at the age of 77, he had reconciled himself to being a dying man whose life had been, in a sense, a failure.

But a strong self-image is essential for any real achievement. Bernard Shaw recognised that clearly and set out to create one from an early stage. Only his first novel IMMATURITY — written when he was 23 and unpublished for half a century — has the kind of vague, indeterminate hero we find in Wells. Then Shaw produced a series of novels in each of which he experiments with a new self-image, a hero possessed of inner-certainty and conviction, until he found what he was looking for in Sidney Trefusis, the 'unsocial socialist' in the novel of that title, and stuck with it. And Trefusis would reappear in the form of Shaw's most loquacious and forceful hero John Tanner, in MAN AND SUPERMAN. But Wells never learned the trick, and was stuck with his diffident little cockney until he was too old to change.

The last reincarnation of his cockney hero occurs in one of his most curious and interesting novels, CHRISTINA ALBERTA'S FATHER, published in 1925, when Wells was nearly sixty. Mr Preemby is another of Wells's modest little nonentities, who differs from Kipps and Mr Polly in suddenly deciding that he is more important than he had assumed. At a mock-séance in Tunbridge, someone pulls his leg by telling him that he is the incarnation of Sargon, the king of Sumeria; he then decides it is his destiny to bring peace to the world and free humankind from poverty and oppression. After wandering away from home and calling disciples, he is arrested, certified and placed in an asylum. He dies a few weeks after being rescued from it.

But this is not really a novel about a harmless little man going mad. Like Kipps and Polly, Preemby has always kept his imagination alive with books about Atlantis and the secrets of the pyramids and ancient Tibet. So what happens to him when he is told that he is a reincarnation of Sargon is a kind of awakening, such as happens to Mr Polly when he sets the house on fire and realises 'If you don't like your lie you can change it' (a phrase that, in my teens, led me to leave home and take to the road.) Wells is saying that people like Mr Polly and Preemby *do not know who they are.* The one certain thing is that they are not Mr Polly and Preemby. And since Wells believes that, since the end of the Great War, mankind had entered a new phase, he feels that Preemby is one of any who are awakening to new consciousness. It is this that makes CHRISTINA ALBERTA'S FATHER in some ways one of his best novels.

Yet it also marked the beginning of a slowly increasing pessimism that would darken his last two decades. We can begin to understand that pessimism by looking at a novel he had written a year earlier, MEN LIKE GODS. Intended as a successor to the earlier A MODERN UTOPIA, this is the story of a group of distinguished people — including Balfour and Churchill — on their way to lunch at Windsor when they find themselves on a strange planet, having apparently passed through some fourth-dimensional window that has been engineered by the 'Utopians'. Wells's picture of this 'ideal society' is, quite simply, unbelievably boring, all sweetness and light and genetics. (Aldous Huxley wrote BRAVE NEW WORLD as a counterblast). Wells had simply failed to grasp that human beings need more than tidily-engineered lives to be happy: that they need some kind of *creative* effort and purpose. In MEN LIKE GODS, that early Wells of the scientific romances has simply run out of steam, and must have been aware of it.

CHRISTINA ALBERTA'S FATHER is an attempt to undo the damage, and return to a novel that has some heart and soul. It would be another ten years before Wells began to see the answer, and that came about in the opening pages of EXPERIMENT IN AUTOBIOGRAPHY. (1934).

He begins: 'I need freedom of mind. I need peace for work. I am distressed by immediate circumstances. My thoughts and work are encumbered by claims and vexations...'

He continues:

'There is nothing I think very exceptional in my situation as a mental worker. Entanglement is our common lot. I believe this craving for a release from—bothers, from daily demands and urgencies, from responsibilities and tempting distractions, is shared by an increasing number of people who, with specialized and distinctive work to do, find themselves eaten up by first-hand affairs. This is the outcome of a specialization and a sublimation of interests that has become frequent only in the last century or so. Spaciousness and leisure, and even the desire for spaciousness and leisure, have so far been exceptional. Most individual creatures since life began, have been "up against it" all the time, have been driven continually by fear and cravings, have had to respond to the unresting antagonisms of their surroundings, and they have found a sufficient and sustaining interest in the drama of immediate events provided for them by these demands. Essentially, their living was continuous adjustment to happenings. Good hap and ill hap filled it entirely. They hungered and ate and they desired and loved; they were amused and attracted, they pursued or escaped, they were overtaken and they died.

'But with the dawn of human foresight and with the appearance of a great surplus of energy in life such as the last century or so has revealed, there has been a progressive emancipation of the attention from everyday urgencies. What was once the whole of life has become, to an increasing extent, merely the background of life. People can ask now what would have been an extraordinary question five hundred years ago. They can say, "Yes, you earn a living, you support a family, you love and hate, but—what do you do?"

'Conceptions of living, divorced more and more from immediacy, distinguish the modern civilized man from all former life. In art, in pure science, in literature, for instance, many people find sustaining series of interests and incentives which have come at last to have a greater value for them than any primary needs and satisfactions. These primary needs are taken for granted. The everyday things of life become subordinate to these wider interests which have taken hold of them, and they continue to value everyday things, personal affections and material profit and loss, only in so far as they are ancillary to the newer ruling system of effort, and to evade or disregard them in so far as they are antagonistic or obstructive to that. And the desire to live as fully as possible within the ruling system of effort becomes increasingly conscious and defined.

'The originative intellectual worker is not a normal human being and does not lead nor desire to lead a normal human life. He wants to lead a supernormal life.

'Mankind is realizing more and more surely that to escape from individual immediacies into the less personal activities now increasing in human society is not, like games, reverie, intoxication or suicide, a suspension or abandonment of the primary life; on the contrary it is the way to power over that primary life which, though subordinated, remains intact. Essentially it is an imposition upon the primary life of a participation in the greater life of the race as a whole. In studies and studios and laboratories, administrative bureaus and exploring expeditions, a new world is germinated and develops. It is not a repudiation of the old but a vast extension of it, in a racial synthesis into which individual aims will ultimately be absorbed. We originative intellectual workers are reconditioning human life...

'*We are like early amphibians, so to speak, struggling out of the waters that have hitherto covered our kind, into the air, seeking to breathe in a new fashion and emancipate ourselves from long accepted and long unquestioned necessities. At last it becomes for us a case of air or nothing. But the new land has not yet definitively emerged from the waters and we swim distressfully in an element we wish to abandon.* (My italics.)

I do not now in the least desire to live longer unless I can go on with what I consider to be my proper business.'

I feel these are not only the most important words Wells ever wrote, but among the most important words written in the past century.

We can begin to understand the pessimism that gradually crept upon him. He felt that CHRISTINA ALBERTA'S FATHER was the last of his old 'Wellsian' novels, the novels of Wells the story-teller. Now he felt he had to find some new form, which would allow him to speak more directly to the reader. Its beginnings are already plain in CHRISTINA ALBERTA'S FATHER, especially its last chapters. After that, in novels like the vast WORLD OF WILLIAM CLISSOLD, he is earnestly addressing us rather than simply trying to entertain. Novels like THE AUTOCRACY OF MR PARHAM or THE BULPINGTON OF BLUP do not even attempt to compete with the early works. We almost need to call them by a new name – or perhaps borrow Graham Greene's word 'entertainments'. He is still capable of the occasional tremendous parable, like THE CROQUET PLAYER. But his main work is now to be found in books like WHAT ARE WE TO DO WITH OUR LIVES, THE SHAPE OF THINGS TO COME and THE FATE OF HOMO SAPIENS. He wants to show us the way out of a situation that he feels is becoming increasingly dark.

Which is why, in late 1943, when he knew he was becoming increasingly ill, he began THE HAPPY TURNING. It is almost a return to 'The Door in the Wall', with one major difference. That story had been romantically pessimistic. The successful politician yearns for what he feels he abandoned. (In that respect it reminds us of Orson Welles's CITIZEN KANE.) But now Wells feels he is near the end, and he is still facing that irritating loss of privacy as when he was writing the EXPERIMENT IN AUTOBIOGRAPHY. But at least he finds that his dream life is offering him a kind of 'door in the wall'. So he permits himself to fantasize about 'a day when a cleansed and liberated world will take the Happy Turning in good earnest and pass out of the base and angry conflicts that distract us from whole-some living'.

Ever since those early days of ANTICIPATIONS (1901), Wells had seen himself as the social scientist who would design the world's future Now, in 1945, it seemed that politicians and militarists had ruined that future, and there was little left to hope for. In the deep depression, Wells allowed himself to feel that in the past few months, some fundamental change had taken place, so that 'the end of everything we call life is close at hand, and cannot be evaded. A frightful queer-ness has come into life'. It is, he says, as if the force of gravitation has disappeared from the solar system, so everything is flying apart.

It sounds not unlike Yeats' 'Second Coming': 'Things fall apart, the centre cannot hold'. But then, Yeats went on to write that great final poem 'Under Ben Bulben', in which he recognises that the answer lies in that slow march of human evolution, whose aim is 'profane perfection of mankind', so that even globe-trot-ting tourists can feel its power as they look at the Sistine Chapel ceiling. And Yeats understood something that Wells failed to grasp: that in certain moments of illumination, man suddenly 'completes his partial mind. Our minds are like the moon in its last quarter; yet, although invisible, the remaining three quarters are there all the time.' The answer, Yeats realised, lies in the mind *itself.*

Yet Wells himself had shown his instinctive grasp of the same insight when he wrote: 'The bird is a creature of the air, the fish is a creature of the water, man is a creature of the mind'. Whatever his faults as a writer or human being, that sentence is enough to establish him as one of the greatest minds of modern times.

THE
HAPPY
TURNING

I
How I Came to the Happy Turning

I AM DREAMING FAR more than I did before this chaotic war invaded my waking hours. My days are now wholly full of war effort: What can I do? What ought I to do? Where is the next opportunity and what dangers gather ahead? I am urgent. I overstrain. And now something deep within me protests and rebels, and says: "These war-makers have yoked and enslaved you. You are defeated if you give yourself wholly to war."

I answer evasively: "Presently I will relax."

That serves in the daytime but not at night. I take care to keep as fit as I can and not to let my war preoccupations develop into the nervous waste of anxiety. I never dream about war. I dream neither of its horrors nor its strategy. When I sleep, a more adult and modern and civilized part of my being comes into play. More and more are my dreams what I believe the psychologists call compensatory; the imaginations I have suppressed revolt and take control.

Some time ago I dreamt a dream that recurs with variations again and again, so that it is a sort of Open Sesame for all my excursions into dreamland. In my daytime efforts to keep myself fit and active, I oblige myself to walk a mile or so on all days that are not impossibly harsh. I walk to the right to the Zoo, or I walk across to Queen Mary's Rose Garden or down by several routes to my Savile Club, or I bait my walk with Smith's bookshop at Baker Street. I have to sit down a bit every now and then, and that limits my range. I've played these ambulatory variations now for two year and a half, for I am too busy to go out of town, out of reach of my books, and my waking self has never uttered a protest. But now the—what do they call it?—subliminal consciousness?—has in the most charming way asserted my unformulated desire, with this dream, which I will call the dream of the Happy Turning.

I dream I am at my front door starting out for the accustomed round. I go out and suddenly realize there is a possible turning I have overlooked.

Odd I have never taken it, but there it is! And in a trice I am walking more briskly than I ever walked before, up hill and down dale, in scenes of happiness such as I have never hoped to see again. At first the Turning itself was the essence of the dream. Now, directly my dream unfolds I know where I am; it has become a mere key to this delightful land of my lifelong suppressions, in which my desires and unsatisfied fancies, hopes, memories and imaginations have accumulated inexhaustible treasure.

For the first time in my existence I realize what it is to have possession of an entirely healthy and balanced body. I was born astigmatic and in those days nobody bothered about common children's eyes. I could never be sure of bowling a straight ball, and when I jumped down I hit the ground too soon or too late. I was under-nourished and tuberculous, so that I was a skinny puny youth, easily fatigued. Tolerable health came only in my thirties. Muscular precision and hardiness I shall never know in my waking life. But now, beyond the Happy Turning, I leap gulfs unerringly, scale precipices, shin up trees and am indefatigable. There are no infections there; no coughs, no colds; to cough or sneeze would be to wake up and tumble back headlong into those unhygienic present-day realities where dirt-begotten epidemics have their way with us. Maybe a day will come when a cleansed and liberated world will take the Happy Turning in good earnest and pass out of the base and angry conflicts which distract us from wholesome living. All such liberations are possible beyond the Turn. Now I count it good fortune that I can even dream of the gay serenity of that Beyond.

The Happy Turning leads to a world where distance is abolished. Certain phrases—parroted phrases empty of belief—are already to be found in the newspapers and speeches—the abolition of war, the abolition of distance, the abolition of competition and social inequality. But after people have repeated a phrase a great number of times, they begin to realize it has meaning and may even be true. And then it comes true. Beyond the Happy Turning these phrases are realities; hopes fulfilled.

II
SUPPRESSIONS AND SYMBOLISM
IN DREAMLAND

B UT THE FANTASIES of dreamland go an immeasurable way beyond what is now conceivable and practical.

The subliminal self is never straightforward. It awakens us,
for example, to sex and the social reactions of adolescence in the queer-
est, most roundabout way. There are sound biological explanations why
our minds should work in this fashion, but I cannot go into them now.
The submerged intervener is cryptic and oracular; it hints and perplexes.
Symbols become persons and persons symbols; individuals, animals, in-
stitutions, amalgamate and divide and change into one another.

Religions are such stuff as dreams are made of. The Athanasian Creed
is severely logical in dreamland, Isis is transfigured into Hathor, a cow,
Quannon, the crescent moon and Murillo's Queen of Heaven, and still
the dream flows on. Osiris becomes his own son Horus, who becomes
again Osiris and the Virgin Mother, in incessant rotation. This is the
atmosphere of this uncontrollable Wonderland beyond the Turn, in which
my accumulated loves and suppressions, disappointments and stresses,
find release. But very plainly it is my personal needs that provide the
substance of the stories with which my dreaming self now consoles and
regales me.

In the past I do not recall dreams as a frequent factor in my existence,
though some affected me very importantly. As a child I used to have a
sort of geometrical nightmare as if a mad kaleidoscope charged down
upon me, and this was accompanied by intense distress. I may have been
very young then, because I cannot remember how I awakened or whether
I conveyed my distress to anyone. Nor have I ever come upon a description of that dream as happening to any other child.

But I remember a considerable number of quite frightful dreams that
came before my teens. I read precociously, and I was pursued implacably,
to a screaming and weeping awakening, by the more alarming animals
I read about. An uncle from the West Indies described some frightful

spiders that scratched and crawled. I was then put to bed alone in the dark in the upstairs bedroom of a strange house, and I disgraced myself by screaming the house down.

I had horror dreams of torture and cruelty. One made me an atheist. My mother was a deeply religious woman, but she did her best to conceal the Devil from me; there were pictures in an old prayer-book showing hell well alight, but she obliterated these with stamp paper which I was only partially successful in removing, so that until I held the page up to the light, hell was a mere suspicion. And one day I read a description in an old number of CHAMBER'S JOURNAL of a man being broken on the wheel over a slow fire, and in my sleep it flared up into immeasurable disgust. By a mental leap which cut out all intermediaries, the dream artist made it clear that if indeed there was an all powerful God, then it was he and he alone who stood there conducting this torture. I woke and stared at the empty darkness. There was no alternative but madness, and sanity prevailed. God had gone out of my life. He was impossible.

From that time on, I began to invent and talk blasphemy. I do not like filth. Merely dirty stories disgust me, and when sexual jokes have an element of laughter in them almost always it is dishonouring and cruel laughter. But theology has always seemed to me an area for clean fun that should do no harm to any properly constituted person. Blasphemy may frighten unemancipated minds, but it is unbecoming that human beings should be governed by fear. From first to last I have invented a considerable amount of excellent blasphemy. ALL ABOARD FOR ARARAT is the last of a long series of drawings and writings, many of which have never seen and probably never will see the light of print. There must be lingering bits of belief in order to produce the relief of laughter, and such jests may fade out very rapidly at no very distant date.

Only a few other dreams stuck in my memory before I discovered the Happy Turning, and mostly they were absurd and misleading freaks of fantasy. I dreamt my mother was ill and in great distress and wrote off post haste to her. There was nothing at all the matter with her.

I must have had anxiety dreams when I was over-working, in which everything was at sixes and sevens, I must have had them because I devised a technique for dealing with them. Directly I woke up, I got up and dismissed them. I trained myself to make tea and set to work soberly in a dressing-gown, and soon everything fell back into its place and the disturbance succumbed to fatigue and natural sleepiness. My friend J. W. Dunne, who wrote AN EXPERIMENT WITH TIME, lost himself for a time in a Serial Universe and has come back a most delightful writer of fantastic tales, induced me to keep a notebook at my bed-head and jot down my dreams fresh and hot. I do not remember making a note. I just woke up, and whatever dreams may have been hanging about vanished unimportantly forthwith.

So my present resort to dreamland is a new experience. I am a happy explorer telling of a delightful world he has come upon, beyond expectation.

III
Compensation Beyond the Happy Turning

THE SCENERY OF my dreamland is always magnificent or exquisite or otherwise delightful. I should not note it if it were not, and I find dear and delightful people I had never hoped to see again, happy and welcoming. Sometimes they are just themselves for a time, sometimes they are agreeably blended with other people, and at any moment they may see fit to impersonate someone else and cease to be whatever they began by being.

Nobody is dead in this world of release, and I hate nobody. I think that this absence of hate may be very recent. It may be due to my subconscious revolt against the unavoidable hates, disputes, suspicions and conflicts of our daily life in this war. Or it may be that with advancing years a mellowing comes to the mind with the attenuation of ambitions and rivalries. They matter so little at seventy-seven. Both factors, the normal one and this abnormal one of war conditions, may be contributing to my escape.

My waking life is now one of very fierce and definite antagonisms. I feel that the generations ahead may be cheated of much or all of the huge emancipations that could and should follow upon this world storm of fighting; and that ancient and evil organizations and traditions and the necessity common minds are under to believe they have natural inferiors, of whom they are entitled to take advantage, may frustrate all our hopes. I am compelled to spend my utmost energy in warfare against these things.

Dreamland is in flat contradiction to all this distressful strain. Nothing of these conflicts pursues me beyond the Happy Turning. At the Happy Turning is a recognizable Holy Water Stoup which has somehow identified itself with Truth, and in my Dreamland there is not the slightest difficulty about dipping a finger and sprinkling the Holy Catholic Church, or whatever ugly menace to mankind happens to be upon my heels, with it. Whereupon the evil I fear and fight here with all my strength, explodes with a slightly unpleasant odour, and vanishes. Why did I let my heart be troubled? Why was I afraid?

IV
The Holy Carnival

NOTHING DISTRESSFUL TO me can clamber over that Threshold now. But anything and everything that shows me deference may play its part in my relaxation. I have had some very entertaining divine conferences. The gods men worship are difficult to assemble and impossible to count, because of their incorrigible habit of dissolving spasmodically into one another. I have remarked already upon the permutations and combinations, if those words are permissible, of Isis, the original Virgin Mary. Cleopatra's infinite variety was nothing to it. The tangle of the Trinities is even more fantastically versatile. There is the Athanasian Trinity and the Arian Trinity, the Catholic and the Orthodox, the Logos and that ever ambiguous Virgin. There is the Gnostic Godhead, which makes Jehovah out to be the very Devil, and Pope's consolidated Deity:

> "Father of all, in every age
> in every clime adored,
> By Saint, by Savage and by Sage,
> Jehovah, Jove or Lord."

The vast theogony galumphs about in an endless confusion of identities with a stern transcendent solemnity that never deserts it. "Which except a man believe faithfully, he cannot be saved."

A few such cries are uttered with an air of profound significance; a considerable amount of thunder goes on, a crackle of miracles, but never a laugh. To laugh is to awaken.

And in and out and round about this preposterous dance of the divinities, circulates an innumerable swarm of priests and prophets and teachers, wearing the oddest of robes and garments, mitres, triple crowns, scarlet hats, coquettish hoods. No Carnival gone mad can compare with this insane leaping and tumbling procession. They pour endlessly through the streets of my dreamland; striking strange symbolic attitudes, some with virgin beards, some grotesquely shaven and shorn, hunchbacked with copes, bellowing strange chants, uttering dark sayings—but always incredibly solemn. They tuck up their petticoats, these grave elderly gentlemen, and one, two, three, leap gulfs of logic.

I noted the present Primate, chief now of the English order of primates, his lawn sleeves like the plump wings of a theological Strassburg goose, as, bathed in the natural exudations of a strenuous faith, he pranced by me, with the Vatican a-kicking up ahind and afore, and a yellow Jap a-kicking up ahind old Pope. I had a momentary glimpse of the gloomy Dean, in ecstatic union with the Deity, yet contraceptive as ever, and then, before I could satisfy a natural curiosity, a tapping delirium of shrilling cymbals swept him away, "Glory!...Glory!... ALLELUIA!..."

As, on the verge of awakening, I watch this teeming disorder of the human brain, which is always the same and increasingly various, I listen for one simple laugh, I look for one single derisive smile. Always I encounter faces of stupid earnestness. They are positively not putting it on, unless earnest self-deception had become second nature. They are not pretending to be such fools. They *are* such fools...

There is this phase between dreaming and awakening, there is a sense of rapidly intensifying conflict and strain before the straining catgut snaps—exactly as it snaps when we come out of anaesthesia. The Brocken Witches' Sabbath begins dispersing and dissolving, becomes a wildly spinning whirl. Will there be enough broomsticks for everybody? Hi broomstick! Are you engaged, broomstick? That's *my* broomstick. They all leap for the nearest one. They rush to and fro about me and through me, terrified at the Berlioz clangor that heralds the night of the Gods. The Archbishop, Inge, His Holiness, Rabbis, thrust about me. They spin up towards the zenith colliding and fighting among themselves—serious to the end.

Cosmo Gordon Lang, I remark, gets into theological difficulties with his steed, which rears and throws him. There is a wild struggle in which his broomstick vanishes. Down he goes, legs and arms and robes, cartwheeling faster and faster. The dream becomes a religious hailstorm. Whiz, whiz, they come pelting.

I have a vague idea I ought to put up an umbrella. Umbrella?

I laugh and am awake.

V

JESUS OF NAZARETH
DISCUSSES HIS FAILURE

1.

THE COMPANION I find most congenial in the Beyond is Jesus of Nazareth. Like everything in Dreamland he fluctuates, but beyond the Happy Turning his personality is at least as distinct as my own. His scorn and contempt for Christianity go beyond my extremest vocabulary. He was, I believe, the putative son of a certain carpenter, Joseph, but Josephus says his actual father was a Roman soldier named Pantherus. If so, Jesus did not know it.

He began his career as a good illiterate patriotic Jew in indignant revolt against the Roman rule and the Quisling priests who cringed to it. He took up his self-appointed mission under the influence of John the Baptist, who was making trouble for both the Tetrarch in Galilee and the Roman Procurator in Jerusalem. John was an uncompromising Puritan, and the first thing his disciples had to do, was to get soundly baptized in Jordan. Then he seemed to run out of ideas. After their first encounter John and Jesus went their different ways. There was little discipleship in Jesus.

He played an inconspicuous role in the Salome affair, and he assures me he never baptized anybody. But he was brooding on the Jewish situation, which he felt needed more than moral denunciation and water. He decided to get together a band of followers and march on Jerusalem. Where, as the Gospel witnesses tell very convincingly, with such contradictions as are natural to men writing about it all many years later, the sacred Jewish priests did their best to obliterate him. He learnt much as he went on. He seems to have said some good things and had others imputed to him. He became a sort of Essene Joe Miller. He learnt and changed as he went on.

Gods! how he hated priests, and how he hates them now! And Paul! "Fathering all this nonsense about being 'The Christ' on *me* of all people! Christian! He started that at Antioch. I never had the chance of a straight talk to him. I wish I could come upon him some time. But he never seems to be here... There are a few things I could say to him," said Jesus reflectively, and added, "Plain things..."

I regretted Paul's absence.

"One must draw the line somewhere," I said. In this happy place, Paul's in the discard."

"Yes," reflected Jesus, dismissing Paul; "there were such a lot of things I didn't know, and such a lot of snares for the feet of a man who feels more strongly than he understands. I see so plainly now how incompetently I set about it."

He surveyed his shapely feet cooling in the refreshing greensward of Happyland. The stigmata were in evidence, but not obtrusively so. They were not eyesores. They have since been disgustingly irritated and made much of by the sedulous uncleanness of the saints.

"*Never* have disciples," said Jesus of Nazareth. "it was my greatest mistake. I imitated the tradition of having such divisional commanders to marshal the rabble I led to Jerusalem. It has been the common mistake of all world-menders, and I fell into it in my turn as a matter of course. I had no idea what a real revolution had to be; how it had to go on from and to and fro between man and man, each one making his contribution. I was just another young man in a hurry. I thought I could carry the whole load, and I picked my dozen almost haphazard.

"What a crew they were! I am told that even these Gospels you talk about, are unflattering in their account of them.

"There is nothing flattering to be told about them. What a crew to start upon saving the world! From the first they began badgering me about their relative importance...

"And their *stupidity!* They would misunderstand the simplest metaphors. I would say, 'The Kingdom of Heaven is like so-and-so and so-and so'...In the simplest terms...

"They always got it wrong.

"After a time I realized I could never open my mouth and think aloud without being misunderstood. I remember trying to make our breach with all orthodox and ceremonial limitations clear beyond any chance of relapse. I made up a parable about a Good Samaritan. Not *half* a bad story."

"We have the story," I said.

"I was sloughing off my patriotism at a great rate. I was realizing the Kingdom of Heaven had to be a universal thing. Or nothing. Does your version go like that?"

"It goes like that."

"But it never altered their belief that they had come into the business on the ground floor."

"You told another good story about some Labourers in the Vineyard."

"From the same point of view?"

"From the same point of view."

"Did it alter their ideas in the least?"

"Nothing seemed to alter their ideas in the least."

"It was a dismal time when our great March on Jerusalem petered out. You know when they got us in the Garden of Gethsemane I went to pieces completely... The disciples, when they realized public opinion was against them, just dropped their weapons and dispersed. No guts in them. Simon Peter slashed off a man's ear and then threw away his sword and pretended not to know me...

"I wanted to kick myself. I derided myself. I saw all the mistakes I had made in my haste. I spoke in the bitterest irony. Nothing for it now but to know one had had good intentions. '*My* peace,' I said, 'I give unto you.'

"The actual crucifixion was a small matter in comparison. I was worn out and glad to be dying, so far as that went, long before those two other fellows—I forget who they were. One was drunk and abusive. But being crucified upon the irreparable things that one has done, realizing that one has failed, that you have let yourself down and your poor silly disciples down and mankind down, that the God in you has deserted you—that was the ultimate torment. Even on the cross I remember shouting out something about it."

"Eli. Eli, lama sabachthani?" I said.

"Did someone get that down?" he replied.

"Don't you read the Gospels?"

"Good God, *No!*" he said. "How *can* I? I was crucified before all that."

"But you seem to know how things have gone?"

"It was plain enough how they were going."

"Don't you," I asked rather stupidly, forgetting where we were, "keep yourself informed about terrestrial affairs?"

"They crucify me daily," he said. "I know that. Yes."

2.

Then without any sign of compunction, with that easy inconsistency which is so natural in the Dreamland atmosphere, he dropped the pose of knowing nothing of the Gospels and began to discuss them with the acutest penetration. He experimented with one explanation.

"People get here, good religious gentle beings, bringing the books they believe in. I talk to them because they are often so right-hearted that it perplexes me to find how wrong-headed they can be.

"Though I saw things going wrong after my crucifixion..."

That was not good enough. He went further and re-told the story of the Resurrection...

"I saw that fellow Paul. That story is quite true. I fainted but I didn't die, and that dear old Joseph of Arimathea put me away in his own private sepulcher. Matthew's Gospel exaggerates about its being sealed and watched, and Mark, Luke and John came nearer the facts. I was put away by Joseph and Nicodemus, among a lot of spices and comforts, there was food and wine and fruit and even some money, and when I awoke I was disgusted beyond measure to realise I was not dead. I sat there eating, because I was exhausted, and wondering what I had best do. Perhaps after all our Heavenly Father had a use for me, and, like yourself, I have never been willing to die. I would just obliterate myself for a time and think things over. You know something of that feeling."

"All my life," I said.

"Of course I ran up against some of the old set. There's no end of circumstantial truth in the gospels. Some of the women were hanging about the garden where I had been deposited. I didn't know what to say to them. I had no clear idea of the next step to take. I still felt there was much to be said and done in spite of the jumble I had made of it all. 'I must go away,' I said. "Whither I go you cannot come. Stick to my teachings, and when I come back we'll have it all gloriously right.'

"Old Thomas thought I was a ghost, and he had to feel the nail holes in my hands before he would believe.

"I met two of them in an inn where I had gone for a bite, and we ate together. Gradually I got away from them as I worked my way north, to think things over from the beginning; while they got together to wait for the Second Coming.

"I was never much of a linguist—no Pentecost for me and so I couldn't go far into Syria beyond the range of my native Galilee."

"You didn't speak Hebrew?"

"Nobody *spoke* Hebrew in my time. Not a soul. It was a dead language. We used to read the Pentateuch and some of the prophets in the synagogues in Hebrew, and the scholars in Jerusalem kept up the cult, but the sort of Hebrew I knew was almost on a level with the rote-learnt Latin a provincial priest would gabble in the early Dark Ages before the Benedictines bucked up classical learning. A majority of Jews, in Egypt for example, knew the Scriptures only through the Septuagint translation. When I got up and read the Law in the Nazareth synagogue, they realized my limitations and threw me out. This Aramaic we talked carried one far into Syria and along the coasts. So that I would wander away again when the Christians made trouble.

"I was not a bad carpenter, slow but careful and accurate. I rather liked Antioch—it was big place in which one could lose oneself—if only Paul hadn't had a way of turning up there and asserting that I was the Son of the Holy Ghost. I knew there were some odd stories about mother. But you see I had every opportunity of hearing Paul on the top of his form. It was no good interrupting him. He would have bawled me out at once. And before I had thought out my problem, I died. I forget my last illness; some form of malaria, I think, and where my body is buried I haven't the faintest idea..."

"Not in the Holy Sepulchre?"

He smiled the Crusades away.

"And that's the true life and story of Jesus of Nazareth, the world's greatest failure?"

3.

He began to change again. He smiled that charming confidential smile of his, which commonly preceded his leg-pulling phase, and then he became a different Jesus altogether, something much more Evangelical, the Pastor of a renascent City Temple perhaps. I did not know how to prevent that. You cannot dictate to a dream. He became—business-like. He escaped into the impossible.

"I don't know where you get your press cuttings," said this transfigured Jesus. "The stuff these infernal Christians pour out! I don't read a tenth of it."

Jesus of Nazareth reading press cuttings! "But *could* you *read?*" I protested, and woke up, before he could explain, as I know this metamorphosed Redeemer would have done, that he had been learning, learning.

But except for Dreamland the dead are finished and done. We have Holy Writ for it. My Jesus used to be fond of saying "It is written", but had that Jesus ever heard a single quotation from Ecclesiastes—with its stern insistence upon human finality?....

"A living dog is better than a dead lion... The dead know not anything... There is no work, nor device, nor knowledge, nor wisdom, in the grave, whither thou goest."

VI
THE ARCHITECT PLANS THE WORLD

B UT THAT CARNIVAL of the Gods and those bishops on broomsticks and that heart to heart talk about the difficulties of world-mending with one of its most celebrated failures, are just two among my endless adventures in Dreamland, and I do not know from night to night what new refreshment awaits me.

There is a lot of architecture beyond there. Sometimes I dream of a purely architectural world. But that architecture goes far beyond the mere putting-up of buildings and groups of buildings here and there. The architects of Dreamland lay out a whole new world. Their gigantic schemes tower to the stratosphere, plumb the depths of the earth, groom mountains, divert ocean currents and dry up seas. My identity merges inextricably with every dreamland architect. "We" do this; "we" do that. We share a common excitement at every fresh idea.

The agronomes—there are no farmers in Dreamland—come along and tell us, "We can produce all the food and the best of food and the most delightful of food, not to mention all the drinks that make glad the heart of man, most easily and expeditiously for your happy thousands of millions, in those few hundred thousand square miles we have marked out upon this globe for you, and the rest of the planet you can have to live in and make homes of and gardens of and playgrounds and—slightly controlled—wildernesses, and everything you architects can dream of and devise."

The geographers and metallurgists and mineralogists and engineers unfold their possibilities to us. "This is what you will be wise to do," they will say, "and this you can do if you will, and it is for you architects to see that none of our mines and pits become eyesores and offences against the ever acuter sensibilities of mankind," and forthwith we shall sit down with them and draw and redraw our plans. The artists will come demanding surfaces to decorate; the musicians will demand great sound-proof auditoria, so that those who want to hear can hear and no one be bothered by unsolicited noise. All roads lead to architecture and building and re-building. These things We, the Creative King in Man, will carry out and carry on.

In these dreams I apprehend gigantic facades, vast stretches of mag-nificently schemed landscape, moving roads that will take you wherever you want to go instead of your taking them. "All this We do and more also," I rejoice. And though endless lovely new things are achieved, noth-ing a human heart has loved will ever be lost. I find myself a child again, the town-bred child I was, rejoicing in the sounds and sights of a coun-try lane, delighting in by-ways where the honeysuckle twines about the ragged robin and one picks and nibbles the bread and cheese buds. Or one creeps through a hedge, conquering its resistance, into a tactfully unguarded garden where there are white raspberry canes and half-ripe gooseberries, black cherries and greengages. And then back to the grown-up magnificence once more...

Old fruits there are in Dreamland, but we feast on many marvelous new ones also. There is a vast Luther Burbank organization at work upon them. And in these latter days, as the war effort strains our lives towards greater and greater austerity, there has been a notable increase of feasting and banqueting in my Dreams. We sit long at table, for there is time for everything where time ceases. I will not tantalize you with my last menu...

I cannot set any of these things down in sketches and forecasts and de-tailed descriptions, for how can I foretell what a hundred million brains, all better than mine, will conceive and plan and replan and continually enhance—they dissolve and vanish as I wake, but in my dream, I dream they are delightful beyond all experience, and, with that, Dreamland is satisfied.

VII
MIRACLES, DEVILS AND
THE GADARENE SWINE

1.

"THESE ARE THE unavoidable distresses of a sick world. There is no way out of it. Every human being is a poisoned human being. We are all infected. A thousand contagions are in our blood. There is no health in us."

"And no magic remedy," we agree.

"Baptism? So natural and obvious to turn to that, and just symbolize our cleansing. So natural for poor infected things to hope and seek for Healers and Leaders to Well Being. So hard to tell them that there is no Salvation but in and through themselves."

"They used," said Jesus, detaching himself a little from me, "to crowd upon me—just as they would have crowded upon any passing novelty, gaping for me to do the tricks they called miracles. A lot of them were bed-rid malingerers and lazy spiritless people, but when I told them to get up and walk, with a threat in my eye, they walked all right. Also I made the disciples baptize and wash them. That proved an effective remedy in many cases. I never handled them myself. I've always had a sort of physical fastidiousness. Poor physique, I suppose...

"Beggars with good marketable sores used to get out of my way for fear of exposure. If sympathetic friends caught them and dragged them up to me, they had the alternatives of confessing themselves humbugs, which might have had disagreeable consequences for them, or adding to my thaumaturgic prestige. So they added to my thaumaturgic prestige.

"A lot of people in my time were possessed by devils, talked aloud, muttered queer things, frightened the timid and the children. Once they got that way with their neighbors, it was hard to get out of it. They liked being feared, of course, but they did not liked being shunned and stoned. They appreciated the distinction of being possessed, but it is very inconvenient to be always possessed and never have a quiet moment. They found my stern exorcisms restful and acceptable. But many, when they realized that nobody was taking notice of them, decided after a time to relapse and take unto themselves seven devils, each worse than the first..."

"The Gospels," I said, "are rather vague about that. They read rather as if you were just letting fly at the eagerness with which the enlightened relapse. Did you really believe there *were* devils?"

"Not finally. But at first yes. It was the prevalent idea and people lent themselves to it. There was that absurd affair with the pigs. Where was it?"

"The Gadarene swine? I'd love to hear about that."

"Yes, yes. One of my minor failures.

"The people came and begged me to stop my confounded miracles and get right out of the country as soon as possible. This fellow used to prowl about stark staring naked, exhibiting himself disgustingly, scaring girls and children and assaulting people, howling and cursing and having a great time. At first everyone wanted me to do something about it. And *he* thought I could and would dispossess him. He hid in a graveyard and when he realised I had got him, he came out in tremendous style. No solitary devil possessed him, he howled. Never was a man so bedeviled. He was a whole Legion. There were some pigs feeding near by and he made such an uproar that they took fright and stampeded down a steep place and into the sea. Quite a lot were drowned, and then it was the people came out and begged me to be off. They insisted. They saw me to my boat."

"I'm glad to have the story from you," I said. As you know, the dear old Gospels are at sixes and sevens. Matthew, exaggerating as usual and spoiling his story, says there were *two* madmen, Mark says there was only one and that there were precisely two thousand pigs, while Luke tells a long story of how poor Legion wanted to come away with you out of the country. I can quite understand he felt he might be a bit unpopular... You left him behind."

"He was the aggressive sort of man *anyone* would leave behind," said Jesus. "Gladly."

"And you don't know what became of him?"

"I *think* they went up the hill to look for him after they had seen me off. They were business-like people, those Gadarenes. Whether they got him I don't know. The Gospels, you will have observed, tell nothing about it."

"Well, you had brought away all your Gospel witnesses."

2.

"Those crowds! I used to insist upon the children coming nearest... They smelt—weaker. And they were artless. Yes—... With or without a reason, I loved and pitied these foredoomed sacrifices to life. So long as they were little. It was a queer thing going from place to place, with something very urgent to say, that I knew ought to be said and which I was honestly trying to find words for, and to have to push my way through a smelly press of human degradation... All the time it was: 'Just one *little* miracle! Something we can tell our friends about. Something to *show!'*

"They would ask to have a wart or a whitlow cured—as a souvenir!

"A lot of them who had no luck with me couldn't bear the humiliation. So they went off and invented things. These downright liars just loaded me with wonders, far beyond anything else I did. They had a free hand..."

"That has been the common lot of everyone who felt there was something he ought to say," I remarked. "Everyone. Buddha and St. Benedict, every saint in the calendar is half buried under a cairn of marvel-mongers' lies. Mankind would have smothered itself in its own lies long ago, if history were not so plainly incredible. Truth has a way of heaving up through the cracks of history. Or we should be damned without hope."

3.

We sat digging our toes into the Elysian greensward, reflecting, in the infinite leisure of finished lives, upon our particular failures to release the human thought that still seeks release and realization in time and space.

"Your miracle cadgers remind me of autograph hunters," I remarked.

"Never heard of them," he said. "What are they?"

"They leave you alone at ordinary times, and they haven't the slightest desire to hear a word you have to say at any time, but if you make a lecture or a broadcast, they seem to spring up like flies from offal and buzz about your face. But when you try to tell them the truth of things, they say you are 'preaching' and turn away."

He sat judging his past impartially.

"It was hard not to humbug just a bit to catch their attention... Just *manage* them a bit. Once when I had been feasting in the desert and trying to get my ideas in order, I saw the Devil in a sort of vision."

"Jehovah's Satan?" I asked, delighted. "The actual Tempter?"

"The very Devil. That was how the vision arranged itself. He *was* a brisk plausible conceited ass, a lot subtler than poor old 'Thou-Shalt-have-none-over-Gods-but-me'. He took me up some sort of pinnacle. 'If only you would let me manage things for you,' said he, 'you could do anything you liked with the world—anything. All you have to do is put yourself in my hands as your impresario—and just *say* anything you please.'"

"You said: 'Get thee behind me, Satan.'"

"My expression was more colloquial.

" 'Have your own way,' he said, and vanished, and down I came to find the multitudes, mostly with furtive lunch packets, coming out to look for me. They had no confidence in my power to exalt them above hunger and thirst. They expected miracles, but not that sort, and when they found there was food to burn, they were ashamed of themselves and pretended not to have brought anything. So that again was put down to my miraculous gifts...

"Hard not to take Satan's suggestion and avail oneself of his artful dodges...Just what one must not do. Mankind must learn together and rise together. Mankind is one. We are one."

"Mankind is learning," we said. "*We* have schools here..."

We thought in perfect unison. We had suddenly coalesced.

"Let us go and see them," said we. "They won't notice us. We are just wraiths from the frustrated past. They will walk through us and never know we are there."

VIII
A Hymn of Hate Against Sycamores

ONLY SO MANY hours a day can one work full out, and only for so many may one eat, digest or sleep, and the strange forces that make us what we are, as the price of an efficient discharge of these functions, insist upon certain performances called exercises, whereby we are compelled to scramble up and down steep places, row boats, box, fence, dance, ride oscillating horses, hit balls about, dig in gardens or otherwise provoke our perspiration pores to copious activity—involving immediate change of raiment or rheumatism.

In my efforts to maintain and protect a satisfactory thread of thought and purpose for myself and my species amidst this labyrinth of ridiculous animal servitudes, I have achieved considerable economies of time and energy. One main meal a day is better than several, and all that walking and running about with rackets and golf clubs and ball hitting implements can be eliminated, I find, by concentrating upon one's garden. Man, says Holy Writ, was created by a gardener. He yields to the suggestion very readily.

The honest tradesman retires from business with gardening in his mind; he may take a side interest in bowls or suchlike elderly sports, but it is the officially mild obedient yielding garden that dominates his released imagination. He is still much preoccupied by the endless mischievous waywardness of this new sphere he has acquired, when he in his turn is dibbled out, like so many of his seedlings, in the hope rather than the certainty of a glorious resurrection...

CANDIDE experiences all the variety of life, and disillusioned with everything else, comes back to the service of these smug impostures upon our planet...

I simply follow the disposition of my kind, when, between the comprehensive efforts to restate existence in terms of space-time, that engage my dwindling hours of maximum validity, I turn from the Macrocosm to the microcosm and carry on, with an intensifying interest, a struggle, that under the stresses of our present limitations becomes more and more single-handed and inexpert, against the indisciplines, contradictions and disorders of my awkward squad of shrubs and plants and flowers. It is such a *little* back garden; a garden to be laughed at, a small paved garden with beds on either side which used to be filled with flowering plants by a nurseryman, who replaced them by others when they were over. It never dawned upon me that it was also a Cosmos, until I was left alone with it. But now, trowel in hand, I know there is no real difference except in relative size between my seedling antirrhinums and the Pleiades. They both mock me—in a parallel manner.

And among the many things I have learnt from this microcosm is the incredible fierceness, nastiness and brutality of the Vegetable Kingdom. It feeds greedily upon filth in any form, and its life is wholly given up to torture and murder. It is a common delusion that there is something mild and moral about all this green stuff in which our planet is clothed. It is really a question of the pace at which one sees it. We, the higher animals, scurry through life so fast that we do not note the more deliberate horrors of these plant lives. It is only now and then, in a jungle, or amidst the towering white menace of a burnt or burning Australian forest, that Nature strips the moral veils from vegetation and we apprehend its stark ferocity. I doubt if Voltaire ever came face to face with that garden of his without some intervening help; he wrote the end of CANDIDE and died before he realized the truth.

In this back garden of mine, this little Creation to which I play the Lord, I see seedling, bush and tree attacking each other pitilessly and relentlessly, and in particular I have watched a very delightful little almond-tree I loved, done to death before I could do anything to save it. Nearest of the murderers was a holly-tree which I have now sawn almost to the ground and would have destroyed altogether except that a curious albino sport springs from its root; certain rivals for my affection contributed to the outrage; but the chief of the slaughter gang, and still an ever increasing affliction of all I would keep gentle, healthy and beautiful, is a vast lumping Sycamore that grows in the deserted garden next door to me. Like most of my erstwhile neighbours in this Hanover Terrace, next-door has gone away, but he retains his lease; his abandoned garden is a centre of weed distribution, and before I can get anything done about it, all sorts of authorities have to be consulted, and after that I doubt if it will be possible to find the labour necessary to terminate the ever spreading aggressions of this hoggish arborial monster.

Every day when I go out to look at my garden I shake my fist at it and wish the gift of the evil eye. Every day it grows visibly larger, ignoring my hatred. It is not only my garden it devastates. It is destroying the gardens beyond, which also are now abandoned. There there are laburnums and acacias and many abandoned helpless flowering shrubs and plants, awaiting their doom.

These Sycamores are not even entitled to be called Sycamores; they have assumed the name of a better plant than themselves. Says my OX-FORD ENGLISH DICTIONARY; "It is commonly spoken of with a distinguishing adjective as the 'bastard, base or vulgar' sycamore." The true sycamore, or sycomore, as the Bible has it, was a mulberry- or fig-tree (sycoon = Fig), and the people who bear the name in English are probably immigrants from more classical parts of the world who would have done better to call themselves Mulberries instead of mixing themselves up with this vile blob upon the English landscape. In all that follows, when I write "Sycamore", I do not point at them. This tree of mud has stolen their name, and I invite them to share my hate and indignation.

I am trying to find out what scoundrel first brought these gawky trees to my England and my London. It was the work of a cheapener, a fundamentally dishonest spirit. They grow with great rapidity; they can stand the now diminishing London soot because they have a stolid will to live through anything, no matter what evil ensue. So that to the cheap and nasty building estate practitioner they were easy to pass off as even desirable trees. They were the perfect tree for the suburban jerry-builder. They seed pitilessly, and they disseminate minute irritant hairs very bad for the respiratory passages. In leaf they are as blowsy as tippling charwomen, and even when they are stripped they have as little allure. They are more like the compositions of Vaughan Williams or Eric Coates than anything else I know. They branch out with a stupid elimination of the unexpected. You never say to a sycamore as you do to all good music and all lovable trees; "Of course that sequence is exactly right, but who could have thought of it, before you did it!"

A Sycamore, if you told it that, would be disconcerted and wonder whether it had not made some sort of slip...

Men marry Sycamores and by all our laws they are blameless women. It is no plea for a divorce in this preposterous world of ours that a wife has an infinite want of variety.

Well, there is this dirty, ugly, witless, self-protective tree, blighting London; it is everywhere, and I hear no voice raised against it. The other day I went to see an exhibition of designs for the rebuilding of London, and there I saw Sycamores as men walking, and they were scheming as awful a London of squalid jobbery as it is possible to imagine. They just wanted to grow all over it abundantly, sycamore-fashion. They were too stupid to have an idea of the New World we poor sensitive men dream of extracting from our present disasters. They did not know and they did not care whether the world was to be a world at peace or a world at war, living underground in perpetual fear of blitzkriegs or towering up to the skies, a world of universal free trade or shabby competition. They did not know and they did not care. They had schemes for green belts—mostly of sycamore-trees—and rows and rows of nasty little building estate houses. They were out for jobs, they were unable to imagine any other jobs except squalid enlargements of their own, and the blight of their dullness fell upon me, so that I came home cursing and swearing, to the dismay of passers-by, and now, whenever I look over my garden wall at this vast dreary tree, waving its leaves at me, I see them also. Every morning that tree seems to come nearer to me and overhang me more and more.

The sycamore is a complete repudiation of any belief in an intelligent God. One may perhaps believe in a God who made good and evil, but the creation of these Sycamores, men, women and trees, was just damned stupidity.

I shall fight evil to my last breath because that is my nature, but it is the thought of these Sycamores that brings me nearest to despair.

So let me conclude by cursing Sycamores and all who favour and abet Sycamores and have sycamore elements in their nature, and let me avoid all vulgar and irreligious cursing, and curse strictly in the terms provided in Holy Writ, in the Twenty-eighth Chapter of the Book of Deuteronomy.

Listen all ye of the Sycamore tribe, and thank your lucky stars, Mr Mulberry Sycamore, that it does not apply to you!

I draw a deep breath and indicate the same by a white line.

"Cursed shalt thou be in the city, and cursed shalt thou be in the field.

"Cursed shall be thy basket and thy store.

"Cursed shall be the fruit of thy body, and the fruit of thy land, the increase of thy kine, and the flocks of thy sheep.

"Cursed shalt thou be when thou comest in, and cursed shalt thou be when thou goest out.

"The Lord shall send upon thee cursing, vexation and rebuke, in all that thou settest thine hand unto for to do, until thou be destroyed, and until thou perish quickly; because of the wickedness of thy doings...

"The Lord shall make the pestilence cleave unto thee, until he have consumed thee from off the land, whither thou goest to possess it.

"The Lord shall smite thee with a consumption, and with a fever, and with an inflammation, and with an extreme burning, and with the sword, and with blasting, and with mildew; and they shall pursue thee until thou perish.

"And thy heaven that is over thy head shall be brass, and the earth that is under thee shall be iron.

"The Lord shall make the rain of thy land powder and dust: from heaven shall it come down upon thee, until thou be destroyed...

"And thy carcase shall be meat unto all fowls of the air, and unto the beasts of the earth, and no man shall fray them away.

"The Lord will smite thee with the botch of Egypt, and with the emerods, and with the scab, and with the itch, whereof thou canst not be healed.

"The Lord shall smite thee with madness, and blindness, and astonishment of heart:

"And thou shalt grope at noonday, as the blind gropeth in darkness, and thou shalt not prosper in thy ways: and thou shalt be only oppressed and spoiled evermore, and no man will save thee.

"Thou shalt betroth a wife, and another man shall lie with her: thou shalt build a house, and thou shalt not dwell therein: thou shalt plant a vineyard, and shalt not gather the grapes thereof.

"Thine ox shall be slain before thine eyes, and thou shalt not eat thereof: thine ass shall be violently taken away from thee before thy face, and shall not be restored to thee: thy sheep shall be given unto thine enemies, and thou shalt have none to rescue them.

"Thy sons and thy daughters shall be given unto another people, and thine eyes shall look, and fail with longing for them all the day long: and there shall be no might in thine hand...

"The Lord shall smite thee in the knees, and in the legs, with a sore botch that cannot be healed, from the sole of thy foot unto the top of thine head...

"Thou shalt carry much seed out into the field, and shalt gather but little in; for the locust shall consume it.

"Thou shalt plant vineyards, and dress them, but shalt neither drink of the wine, nor gather the grapes; for the worms shall eat them.

"Thou shalt have olive trees throughout all thy coasts, but thou shalt not anoint thyself with the oil; for thine olive shall cast his fruit.

"Thou shalt beget sons and daughters, but thou shalt not enjoy them; for they shall go into captivity.

"All thy trees and fruit of thy land shall the locust consume.

"The stranger that is within thee shall get up above thee very high; and thou shalt come down very low.

"He shall lend to thee, and thou shalt not lend to him; he shall be the head and thou shalt be the tail.

"Moreover all these curses shall come upon thee, and shall pursue thee, and overtake thee, till thou be destroyed.

"Because thou servedst not the Lord thy God with joyfulness, and with gladness of heart, for the abundance of all things;

"Therefore shalt thou serve thine enemies which the Lord shall send against theee, in hunger, and in thirst, and in nakedness, and in want of all things: and he shall put a yoke of iron upon thy neck, until he shall have destroyed thee.

"And thou shalt eat the fruit of thine own body, the flesh of thy sons and of thy daughters, which the Lord thy God hath given thee, in the siege, and in the straitness, wherewith thine enemies shall distress thee:

"So that the man that is tender among you, and very delicate, his eye shall be evil toward his brother, and toward the wife of his bosom, and towards the remnant of his children which he shall leave:

"So that he will not give any of them of the flesh of his children who he shall eat: because he hath nothing left him in the siege, and in the straitness, wherewith thine enemies shall distress thee in all thy gates...

"Then the Lord will make thy plagues wonderful, and the plagues of thy seed, even great plagues, and of long continuance, and sore sickness, and long continuance.

"Moreover he will bring upon thee all the diseases of Egypt, which thou wast afraid of; and they shall cleave unto thee.

"Also every sickness, and every plague, which is not written in the book of this law, them will the Lord bring upon thee, until thou be destroyed."

That last clause is a magnificent piece of curse drafting. Not a loophole remains.

This, I think, is all that needs to be said about my neighbour's Sycamore in particular and Sycamores and Sycamorism in general. I can imagine nothing more comprehensive. I can add nothing to it. Take it, Mr Sycamore, take it all and be damned to you! And thank the powers of earth and heaven, Mr Mulberry Sycamore, that it is not to you that these words are addressed.

This cursing, let us realize, is the sort of thing the Pope, his Cardinals, the Archbishops, Bishops, priests and deacons, the pious controllers of the B.B.C, and all the Sycamore Groves of canting Christendom, declare they find so good for the soul of man. This is the spirit of the Sacred Book they distribute about the world to teach men love and gentleness.

The plain, if inadvertent, evidence of Holy Writ is that from the beginning, God knew he had made a mess of things and set Himself to savage his Creation. Time after time, he repented that he had made man, and time after time he sent floods and judgments. He seems to have found Creation almost as obdurate and frustrating and exasperating as I do in my garden.

Here in the freedom of Dreamland I recognize and deal with these Christian teachers for the foolish weaklings they are. I refuse to accept this consecrated riff-raff as my moral and mental equals. Clearly they are either knaves or fools or a blend in various proportions of the two, and to treat them as though they were intelligent honest men in this world crisis, becomes a politeness treasonable to mankind.

I find this little outburst a great relief.

(Thank you, God! For if you serve no other purpose in Dreamland you are still admirable to swear by.)

IX
THE DIVINE TIMELESSNESS
OF BEAUTIFUL THINGS

THE OTHER DAY the Happy Turning took me to the sunlit sweetness of the Elysian fields, and sometimes, after the manner of Dreamland, it seemed to me I was talking to a great number of poets, painters, artists, makers of every sort, and sometimes that I was just talking to myself, and the talk was all about the beautiful things that man has got out of this unrighteous world, and whether there can ever be another happy harvest of Beauty, and, if so, what sort of harvest it may be.

A point we found we were all agreed upon was that Beauty is eternal and final, a joy for ever. There is no progress in it and no decline. You cannot go beyond it. You may make replicas of it; you may record and imitate it, you can destroy it for yourself and others, obliterate it and blaspheme it, but you cannot do away with its invincible divinity. Even when it is a lost God, a Beauty is still God, a being in itself, serene, untroubled, above all the accidents of space and time.

But what we had most in mind was this, that there is a definite limit set to the abundance of any particular Beauty. It is discovered, it is revealed, and that is its end. That God has smiled and passed and returns no more. Other Gods may smile in their turn, and they too will pass away.

We cited instances of these immortal visitations.

There was, said a classical scholar, that gracious beauty which was distilled by Hellenic poets and sculptors out of the vast confusion of antique mythology. It has lit this dull world for all its lovers with an inalienable charm. Pan and the dryads haunt the woodlands, the naiads bathe in the stream, Diana steals down the beams of misty silver to Endymion, and eternally amidst the glittering waters, Triton blows his wreathed horn.

"But one thing goes on," said a man who called himself an anthologist, "and that is the creative magic in English poetic creation." Which threw us all into an intricate disputation that carried us over the whole field of English literature and drama and was shot with a flashing multitude of interests and surprises. "There is not one single Goddess here," we agreed, "but a varied sisterhood, and most of these sisters are wantons and have led lives that make the Olympians seem by comparison calm and consistent and at least superficially decorous." Gradually we begin to disentangle the preoccupations of these lively Beauties.

There is that lost Goddess of beautiful English who, with little Latin and less Greek, played with it so delightfully in Shakespearian days and was finally murdered by her Latin lover in a fit of jealousy because she flirted with the far more lively colloquial scullion downstairs. She came to her tragic end before the Stuarts were done for. For a while she lay calm and rigid in death before her ultimate decay. All that Swift and Sterne, Addison and Gray and Gay, albeit they loved her greatly, could achieve was an unexciting pellucid flow. The DUNCIAD is the dirge of a happy lovely language lying dead under a black pall of Hanoverian gutterals.

Dear heart! she left one bastard by philosophy, not a Goddess indeed but a demi-Goddess, the Wordsworthian discovery of the mystical loveliness beneath reality, but for the rest, we Dreamland anthologists asked, what later Beauty of English is worth our keeping? Newdigate prizewinners, pompous and pretentious verse-makers, the massive uninspired industrious professionalism of Tennyson, head expert of the industry, Longfellow doing his level best, and never succeeding, to make Laughing-Water Hiawatha laugh, the fumed oak stuff from the Morris antique shop, the vanity, crudity and unimaginative topicality of that overrated etcher, Blake, the jingling vulgarities of Byron, Martin Tupper, Alfred Noyes, T. S. Eliot, Bridges and the rest of them—as void of the mysterious exaltation of Beauty as a crew of disinherited mourners at a bankrupt's funeral on a wet day. Who in the great world we dream about will delight in any of this later stuff? Have we any use for it at all?

The anthologist did his best. "There are bits," he pleaded, digging nervously in the addled egg, that curate's egg, of later English poetry. "A rose-red city half as old as time," he quoted, but he could not recall the name of the man who produced that one happy line, and then he bethought himself suddenly of Shelley.

He dredged up a few quotable lines, "The earth doth like a snake renew its winter skin outworn." And a fragment of QUEEN MAB.

"Well?" he said.

"You shall have that," I conceded, "though much of Shelley is copious, intellectualized and tedious stuff, last bubbles from the drifting body of the drowned Goddess, and, such as they were, they rose to the surface and broke and vanished a century and a quarter ago. But all the rest was just trying to go on with something that indeed was finished for ever."

It was my Dream, entirely mine for a while; no one said anything more; and thus, having left English poesy for dead, these fluctuating dream Elysians fell to discussing one of the most radiant smiles of another of these—wanton English Beauties—who lived so fast and gaily in those days of literary loveliness, the divine imagination of the MIDSUMMER NIGHT'S DREAM.

There we agreed, was a piece of the magic that can never lose its charm. "Or THE TEMPEST," said someone.

There again we had a culminating finish, something done, for good and all, so that nothing of the same supreme sort could ever be done again. But all through that happy phase of English inspiration beauty flashed and quivered. Brightest among the London Globe galaxy who slapped together plays and poetry which people now call "Shakespeare", was a brilliant youth of that name, who loved all too freely and retired to Stratford on Avon to die untimely, as his final signatures show, in the mute misery of incipient G.P.I. He stood out among them all in his early years, but, quite apart from these distinctive creations, the language was in such a state that hardly anyone could touch it without striking sparks of loveliness, and one must be very heavily erudite to attribute any particular single flash in the collection to this man or that.

And as My Dreamland company talked in Elysium we became aware of a curious unanimity about that respectable triology, the Beautiful, the Good and the True. Dear old Professor Gilbert Murray appeared among the eternal sunlit greenery and was greeted with a respectful murmur. He declared with a defiant flash in his glasses and a note of passion in his voice, that he believed in the Good, the Beautiful and the True, but, before he could be asked any questions, he vanished from among us completely, and we were left to consider what he meant by these words. We found we were agreed that he had put three realities, essentially different in their nature, upon a quasi-equality for which there was no justification whatever.

We left the moral factor, the Good, aside for the present. Goodness is a matter of *mores,* of good social behaviour, and there is so wide a diversity of social values in the world that it seemed unnecessary to my Elysians to question anything so impermanent. The transitoriness of morality is in flat contrast to the deathless finality of beauty.

But when we turned to literature which does not pretend to beauty in the first place, but to interest of statement or narratives, we found something, that only verges, as it were, in a few incidental passages, and by accident, on poetic beauty. For the rest, literature, both the philosophical, the "scientific" and the fictitious, is telling about what things are, what life is; about its excitements, its emotional effects, its expectations, its laughter and tears. It is as different from poesy as apple pie is from Aurora.

This work of the human mind in telling and enforcing a view has produced a huge real literature quite apart from the infinitely vaster sham literature which is foisted upon people whose cacotrophically educated undiscriminating minds cannot even perceive they are being told nothing at all, and who read in a muzzy fashion, as people play patience, because they can think of nothing better to do.

This literature of reality has not the permanence of beauty. It absorbs and reproduces the story-telling and statements of the past. It does its utmost to recapture from the past the experiences swallowed by the maw of time. Or it invents typical or experimental characters to try over problems and variations in conduct. There can be no classical novels or romances. The strictly circumstantial ones last longest. Fielding's VOYAGE TO LISBON will out live TOM JONES. Stories become tedious as our vision broadens. Nor are there classics of science. Knowledge pours in continually to amplify and correct. Yet every new realization, every fresh discovery, has for those who make it, a quality of beauty, transitory indeed but otherwise as clear and pure as that enduring Beauty we cherish for ever, an ephemeral beauty for one man or for a group of mortals, sufficient to make a life's devotion to service of truth worth while.

So we found ourselves in agreement that the human mind may be in a phase of transition to a new, fearless, clear-headed way of living in which understanding will be the supreme interest of life, and beauty a mere smile of approval. So it is at any rate in the Dreamland to which my particular Happy Turning takes me. There shines a world "beyond good and evil", and there, in a universe completely conscious of itself, Being achieves its end.

THE END

                                            ❧   ❧   ❧

MIND AT THE END
OF ITS TETHER

FOREWORD

T HE TWO PAMPHLETS collected here, THE HAPPY TURNING and MIND AT THE END OF ITS TETHER, were H. G. Wells's final publications. He was, respectively, seventy-seven and seventy-nine when he penned these works, and in poor health. He died soon after publishing MIND AT THE END OF ITS TETHER, on August 13, 1946.

Like some others of my generation — I was born in 1946 — I first heard of Wells's final work in THE OUTSIDER, Colin Wilson's study of the literature of alienation (originally published 1956, reprinted Tarcher/Putnam, New York 1982). In his first chapter, Wilson writes that MIND AT THE END OF ITS TETHER "must be considered the most pessimistic single utterance in modern literature." As Wilson's book was the literary guide that got me interested in Jean-Paul Sartre's novel NAUSEA — a personal touchstone — I was of course intrigued by the possibility that the great old SF Master was a heavy existentialist as well.

These last works of Wells frighten me, not only because of what they say, but because of how they're written. Wells rants, inveighs, rambles, self-aggrandizes, repeats himself, and loses the thread of what he's talking about — in spots the performance verges upon the pitiful. Poor old man.

But the work snaps into focus in the first three sections of MIND AT THE END OF ITS TETHER. Very little doddering here. These pages are as shocking as opening one's bedroom door to find — nothing. A hole in space. The Void.

෯   ෯   ෯

When approaching their own deaths, some people fall into what I might call fatalistic synecdoche. They conflate the whole (the world) with the part (themselves), and announce that the world is about to end. I knew an exasperatingly self-centered old man who every few waking minutes during his seven-year final decline would repeat, "We're all dying." He predicted our joint death perhaps a quarter of a million times before finally succumbing.

Yes, we're all going to die — but not at the same time. To view your own death as the end of the entire outer world is rather conspicuously to miss the point. Each time a spent, decaying tree crashes to the forest floor, a hundred new green shoots spring up. Life is a wheel, eternally renewing herself.

This said, there is a precise sense in which one particular "world" ends with a given person X's death; the doomed "world" is the "world-as-X-knew-it." For each of us human X's, the end of the world-as-X-knew-it is indeed coming up. When Jesus told his disciples that the end of the world was coming in their own lifetimes, he was, on a person-by-person basis, correct.

I'm playing intellectual games here, dancing around an unpleasant subject. But in Wells's last months, the horror of death became immediate and experiential. And so he wrote MIND AT THE END OF ITS TETHER, and indulged himself to the hilt in fatalistic synecdoche. The effect is chilling, apocalyptic. Here's a series of quotes from the first section of his grim last testament:

"The cosmic movement of events is increasingly adverse to the mental make-up of our everyday life..." "... a frightful queerness has come into life...something is happening so that life will never be quite the same ..." "... the Antagonist ... which has endured life for so long by our reckoning ... has now turned against it ... implacably to wipe it out ..." " ... [events] go on and on to an impenetrable mystery, into a voiceless limitless darkness, against which [the] obstinate urgency of our dissatisfied minds may struggle, but will struggle only until it is altogether overcome."

The section ends with a hammer-blow that nails the lid upon the coffin: "There is no way out or round or through."

❧ ❧ ❧

Rich and densely woven, the first three sections of MIND AT THE END OF ITS TETHER bear close rereading. As a more plausible alternative to his claim that the world is coming to an end, Wells suggests that the flow of human history is entering a zone beyond which logical extrapolation must fail.

"It was natural for [me] to assume there was a limit set to change, that new things and events would appear, but that they would appear consistently, preserving the natural sequence of life. ... Hitherto events had been held together by a certain logical consistency ... [but] now it is as if ... everything was driving anyhow to anywhere at a steadily increasing velocity ... [and] events now follow one another in an entirely untrustworthy sequence."

The view that the world is on the brink of a unique and radical transition is sometimes called millenarianism. The millenarianists of our early twenty-first century say we're on the verge of a technological Singularity beyond which it is impossible to see. Are they right? Was Wells?

In hindsight, Wells's time seems much of a piece with the rest of human history: wars, atrocities, improving technology, population increase. The usual. Extrapolating, one supposes that even the most dramatic twenty-first events will also come to seem like mere history — when viewed from yet further down the timeline.

Millenarianism is on the one hand a kind of self-aggrandizement: nobody has ever lived in an era as strange as mine! On the other hand, it's an abdication, a failure of the imagination — a failure that must ultimately beset even so great a futurist and scientific romancer as H. G. Wells.

Some notions from twenty-first century philosophy of computer science are apposite. Human history can be thought of as a kind of computation, a rule-like distributed process being carried out within the individual brains of human beings as they react to the physical computations of the physical world. The massed mental computations of humanity add up to a hive-mind.

In the philosophy of computation, we distinguish between predictable and unpredictable computations, and within the subset of the unpredictable ones, we distinguish between those that appear utterly random, and those so-called gnarly ones which generate fleeting illusions of regularity while remaining solidly unpredictable. The weather, a living organism, the motions of a leaf in the wind, your mental processes, a society's hive-mind, global human history — all of these share the property of being gnarly computations: utterly unpredictable, but not random.

It's not the case that absolutely anything can happen at any time. Local determinism holds sway; things happen for reasons; causes lead to effects. But the massed interactions of the hive members produce a human history that appears inscrutably chaotic.

If you become aware of this, it makes you — queasy. You're in a small craft headed for more and still more rapids, and there's no way off the river. For the young, the never-ending ordeal seems a romp, an adventure. For the old, it's fatiguing — and ultimately terrifying.

                            ᔟ   ᔟ   ᔟ

Wells was no hysteric. He was well aware of a distinction between "... his very intermittent and specialized phases as a philosophical enquirer and the normal interests of his life."

So far as he was concerned, his world was about to end, and the future had become utterly unpredictable. He remarks that one's options are to endure such facts or to evade them; "the end will be the same, but the evasion systems involve ... in most cases blind obedience to egotistical leaders, fanatical persecutions, panics, hysterical violence and cruelty."

Noblesse oblige. It's better to face the facts and make the best of the time we have. "[I] would rather our species ended its story in dignity, kindliness and generosity, and not like drunken cowards in a daze or poisoned rats in a sack."

The final three sections of MIND AT THE END OF ITS TETHER are to filler, inserted to bulk the essay to a length sufficient to be published as a pamphlet. I gather from the excellent forward and notes by his son G. P. Wells* that these sections were in fact written a year earlier; they summarize ideas about evolution, culminating with the suggestion that some future beings of our planet might survive the coming cataclysm. (From a twenty-first century standpoint, it seems possible that our inheritors could well be AIs, robots, or some biotech form of artificial life.)

Throughout MIND AT THE END OF ITS TETHER we feel a sense of struggle: Wells's innate vital optimism versus his moment-by-moment knowledge that the end was near. He was conflicted, unsure, groping. But, right to the end, he never let up.

At the very end of he remarks that, as people are "curious, teachable and experimental from cradle to the grave," some of them may indeed succeed in — keeping our civilization going? To hell with that. He's not going to flinch. The final bright flowering of humanity might at best "succeed in seeing life out to its inevitable end."

Going down in flames; with a bang, not a whimper.

ॐ   ॐ   ॐ

— RUDY RUCKER, LOS GATOS, CALIFORNIA, MARCH 12, 2006.

*These can be found in the British Edition of THE LAST BOOKS OF H.G. WELLS published by the H.G. Wells Society.

PREFACE

THIS LITTLE BOOK brings to a conclusive end the series of essays, memoranda, pamphlets, through which the writer has experimented, challenged discussion, and assembled material bearing upon the fundamental nature of life and time. So far as fundamentals go, he has nothing more and never will have anything more to say.

The greater bulk of that research material may now go down the laboratory sink. It is either superseded or dismissed. It will go out of print and be heard of no more.

This applies particularly to a large assemblage of material published under the title of '42 TO '44. This was gathered together in the course of five or six years and finally it was rushed into print; it was published at a prohibitive price, because, although the writer wanted to put certain things on record, he was acutely aware how very provisional his record still was. Now it can fall into oblivion. The quintessence is here in this small and reasonably priced volume, and the author may use some of the documentary material that figured in its predecessors and which in most cases was as sound as it is irrelevant to our fundamental theme, as a sourcebook for critical writing in whatever remnant of time still remains for him. It is factually quite sound and much will be available for study of the DECLINE AND FALL OF MONARCHY AND COMPETITIVE IMPERIAL-ISMS should the writer last out to write that.

'42 TO '44 was thrown together rather hastily because of an ill-advised medical judgment upon his prospect of living. Among the complications of his never very sound body is a fatty degeneration of the heart, which ended the lives of his father, his elder brother, and a long line of their ancestors for a number of generations. The machine stops short and the man drops dead unaware of his death. Instead of telling him to get his weight down, walk slowly upstairs, and avoid needless excitement, the excellent but perhaps overworked professional doctors gave alarming instructions to his heirs to prepare to take over at any time—Heaven knows why, for, in view of these facts, the writer has never bothered about death except in so far as it meant keeping his accounts and testamentary arrangements up to date. His sons, who understood him better than these professional gentlemen, very naturally and properly consulted him, but, not realizing the amazing limitations of medical professionalism, they did so far accept the doctors' warning that he could not last for another year. For a time his only doctor was the brilliant diabetic specialist, Robin Lawrence, who dealt with him as a diabetic. An inherent indisposition to hazard opinions outside his province combined with professional usage to seal his lips upon the question of the writer's general prospects.

'42 TO '44 therefore was flung together in needless haste, and now it is being disarticulated again and what is useful in it distributed. The writer undertook that it should never be cheaper than the huge price he set upon it, and he will now go further and promise that he will do his utmost to prevent its being reprinted at any price whatever. Thereby he hopes that strange indiscriminate creature, the rare book collector, will get his money's worth...

The writer apologises for this lengthy introduction.

He will get this compact book printed as soon as possible and see that it is issued at a price that will bring it within the reach of everybody who wants to read it. It may be difficult, in view of the determined fight of our reactionaries against all lucid ideas, to secure enough paper for a very abundant first edition. He will do his best. He is retaining the copyright to protect the book from mutilation and misquotation, but he will do nothing to deter anyone who cites it fully, fairly and to any extent, from doing so. This general permission can always be verified by writing to him for confirmation.

I
THE END CLOSES IN UPON MIND

THE WRITER FINDS very considerable reason for believing that, within a period to be estimated by weeks and months rather than by aeons, there has been a fundamental change in the conditions under which life, not simply human life but all self-conscious existence, has been going on since its beginning. This is a very startling persuasion to find establishing itself in one's mind, and he puts forward his conclusions in the certainty that they will be entirely inacceptable to the ordinary rational man.

If his thinking has been sound, then this world is at the end of its tether. The end of everything we call life is close at hand and cannot be evaded. He is telling you the conclusions to which reality has driven his own mind, and he thinks you may be interested enough to consider them, but he is not attempting to impose them upon you. He will do his best to indicate why he has succumbed to so stupendous a proposition. His exposition will have to be done bit by bit, and it demands close reading. He is not attempting to win acquiescence in what he has to say. He writes under the urgency of scientific training, which obliged him to clarify his mind and his world to the utmost limit of his capacity.

That book, '42 TO '44, now seems to him merely incidental matter. It is like the remembered shouts of angry people in a train that has passed and gone for ever. His renascent intelligence finds now that we are confronted with strange convincing realities so overwhelming that, were he indeed one of those logical consistent creatures we incline to claim we are, he would think day and night in a passion of concentration, dismay and mental struggle upon the ultimate disaster that confronts our species.

We are nothing of that sort. Whatever dismaying realities our limited reasoning unfolds before us, our normal life is happily one of personal ambitions, affections, generosities, a mixture in nearly every individual of the narrowest prejudices, hates, competitiveness and jealousies with impulses of the most unselfish and endearing quality, bright friendliness, unasked helpfulness; and this, the everyday foreground of our thoughts, will always be sufficiently vivid to outshine any sustained intellectual persuasion of accumulating specific disaster. We live in reference to past experience and not to future events, however inevitable.

It requires an immense and concentrated effort of realization, demanding constant reminders and refreshment, on the part of a normal intelligence, to perceive that the cosmic movement of events is increasingly adverse to the mental make-up of our everyday life. It is a realization the writer finds extremely difficult to sustain. But while he holds it, the significance of Mind fades. The secular process loses its accustomed appearance of a mental order.

The word "secular" he uses here in the sense of the phrase *"in sæcula saeculorum"*, that is to say, Eternity. He has come to believe that that congruence with mind, which man has attributed to the secular process, is not really there at all. The secular process, as he now sees it, is entirely at one with such non-mental rhythms as the accumulation of crystalline matter in a mineral vein or with the flight of a shower of meteors. The two processes have run parallel for what we call Eternity, and now abruptly they swing off at a tangent from one another—just as a comet at its perihelion hangs portentous in the heavens for a season and then rushes away for ages or for ever. Man's mind accepted the secular process as rational and it could not do otherwise, because he was evolved as part and parcel of it.

Much of this, by and by, the writer has set out in a little book with the grandiose title, THE CONQUEST OF TIME, which Messrs. C. A. Watts and Co. published for him in 1942. Such conquering as that book admits is done by Time rather than Man. *Tempus edax rerum.*

> "Time like an ever rolling stream
> bears all its sons away,
> They fly forgotten as a dream
> dies at the opening day."

But hitherto other sons have appeared, and now only does life pass plainly into a phase of complete finality, so that one can apprehend and anticipate its end.

The reality glares coldly and harshly upon any of those who can wrench their minds from the comforting delusions of normality to face the unsparing question that has overwhelmed the writer. They discover a frightful queerness has come into life. Even quite unobservant people now are betraying, by fits and starts, a certain wonder, a shrinking and fugitive sense that something is happening so that life will never be quite the same again.

Foremost in this scrutiny is the abrupt revelation of a hitherto unsuspected upward limit to quantitative material adjustability. Spread out and examine the pattern of events, and you will find yourself face to face with a new scheme of being, hitherto unimaginable by the human mind. This new cold glare mocks and dazzles the human intelligence, and yet, such is the obstinate vitality of the philosophical urge in minds of that insatiable quality, that they can still, under its cold urgency, seek some way out or round or through the impasse.

The writer is convinced that there is no way out or round or through the impasse. It is the end.

The habitual interest in his life is critical anticipation. Of everything he asks: "To what will this lead?" And it was natural for him to assume that there was a limit set to change, that new things and events would appear, but that they would appear consistently, preserving the natural sequence of life. So that in the present vast confusion of our world, there was always the assumption of an ultimate restoration of rationality, and adaptation and a resumption. It was merely a question, the fascinating question, of what forms the new rational phase would assume, what Overman, Erewhon or what not, would break through the transitory clouds and turmoil. To this, the writer set his mind.

He did his utmost to pursue the trends, that upward spiral, towards their convergence in a new phase in the story of life, and the more he weighed the realities before him the less was he able to detect any convergence whatever. Changes had ceased to be systematic, and the further he estimated the course they were taking, the greater their divergence. Hitherto events had been held together by a certain logical consistency, as the heavenly bodies as we know them have been held together by the pull, the golden cord, of Gravitation. Now it is as if that cord had vanished and everything was driving anyhow to anywhere at a steadily increasing velocity.

The limit to the orderly secular development of life had seemed to be a definitely fixed one, so that it was possible to sketch out the pattern of things to come. But that limit was reached and passed into a hitherto incredible chaos. The more he scrutinized the realities around us, the more difficult it became to sketch out any Pattern of Things to Come.

Distance had been abolished, events had become practically simultaneous throughout the planet, life had to adapt itself to that or perish, and with the presentation of that ultimatum, the Pattern of Things to Come faded away.

Events now follow one another in an entirely untrustworthy sequence. No one knows what to-morrow will bring forth, but no one but a modern scientific philosopher can accept this untrustworthiness fully. Even in his case it plays no part in his everyday behaviour. There he is entirely at one with the normal multitude. The only difference is that he carries about with him this hard harsh conviction of the near conclusive end of all life. That conviction provides no material at all for daily living. It does not prevent his having his everyday affections and interests, indignations and so forth. He is framed of a clay that likes life, that is quite prepared to risk it rather than give way to the antagonistic forces that would break it down to suicide. He was begotten by the will to live, and he will die fighting for life.

He echoes Henley:

> "Out of the night that covers me
> Black as the Pit from pole to pole,
> I thank whatever gods may be
> For my unconquerable soul...
> Beyond this place of wrath and tears
> Looms but the Horror of the shade,
> And yet the menace of the years
> Finds, and shall find, me unafraid."

There, for all his philosophical lucidity, in his invincible sticking to life and his will to live, he parallels the normal multitude, which will carry on in this ever contracting NOW of our daily lives—quite unawake to what it is that is making so much of our existence distressful and evasive and intensifying our need for mutual comfort and redeeming acts of kindliness. He knows, but the multitude is not disposed to know and so it will never know.

The philosophical mind is not what people would call a healthy buoyant mind. That "healthy mind" takes life as it finds it and troubles no more about that. None of us start life as philosophers. We become philosophers sooner or later, or we die before we become philosophical. The realization of limitation and frustration is the beginning of the bitter wisdom of philosophy, and of this, that "healthy mind", by its innate gift for incoherence and piecemeal evasion and credulity, never knows. It takes a priest's assurance, the confident assertion of a leader, a misapplied text—the Bible, bless it! will say any old thing one wants it to say if only one picks out what one needs, or, better, if one lets one's religious comforters pick out the suitable passages—so that one never sees it as a whole. In that invincible ignorance of the dull mass lies its immunity to all the obstinate questioning of the disgruntled mind.

It need never know. The behaviour of the shoal in which it lives and moves and has its being will still for a brief season supply the wonted material for that appreciative, exulting, tragic, pitiful or derisive comment which constitutes art and literature. Mind may be near the end of its tether, and yet that everyday drama will go on because it is the normal make-up of life and there is nothing else to replace it.

To a watcher in some remote entirely alien cosmos, if we may assume that impossibility, it might well seem that extinction is coming to man like a brutal thunderclap of *Halt!*

It never comes like a thunderclap. That *Halt!* comes to this one to-day and that one next week. To the remnant, there is always, "What next?" We may be spinning more and more swiftly into the vortex of extinction, but we do not apprehend as much. To those of us who do not die there is always a to-morrow in this world of ours, which, however it changes, we are accustomed to accept as Normal Being

A harsh queerness is coming over things and rushes past what we have hitherto been wont to consider the definite limits of hard fact. Hard fact runs away from analysis and does not return. Unheard-of strangeness in the quantitative proportions of bulk and substance is already apparent to modern philosophical scrutiny. The limit of size and space shrinks and continues to shrink inexorably. The swift diurnal return of that unrelenting pendulum, the new standard of reference, brings it home to our minds that hard fact is outpacing any standard hitherto accepted.

We pass into the harsh glare of hitherto incredible novelty. It beats the searching imagination. The more it strives the less it grasps. The more strenuous the analysis, the more inescapable the sense of mental defeat. The cinema sheet stares us in the face. That sheet is the actual fabric of Being. Our loves, our hates, our wars and battles, are no more than a phantasmagoria dancing on that fabric, themselves as unsubstantial as a dream. We rage in our dreaming. We may wake up storming with indignation, furious with this or that ineffectual irremovable general, diplomatist, war minister or ruthless exploiter of our fellow men, and we may denounce and indict as righteous anger dictates. '42 TO '44 was made up of that kind of outbreak. But there are thousands of mean, perverted, malicious, heedless and cruel individuals coming into the daylight every day, resolute to frustrate the kindlier purposes of man. In CRUX ANSATA again, this present writer has let himself boil over, freely and violently. Nevertheless it is dream stuff.

"To-morrow, and to-morrow, and to-morrow, creeps in this pretty pace from day to day...and all our yesterdays have lighted fools the way to dusty death...Life...struts and frets his hour upon the stage and then is heard no more...a tale told by an idiot, full of sound and fury, signifying nothing..."

It passes and presently it is vague, indistinct, distorted and at last forgotten for ever.

We discover life in the beginnings of our idiot's recital as an urge to exist so powerful that every form it takes tends to increase in size and numbers and outgrow its supply of food energy. Groups or aggregates or individuals increase not only in numbers but in size. There is an internecine struggle for existence. The bigger aggregations or individual eliminate the smaller and consume more and more. The distinctive pabulum of the type runs short, and new forms, capable of utilizing material which the more primitive were not equipped to assimilate, arises.

This inaugurates a fresh phase in the evolving story of Being. This idiot's tale is not a tale of yesterday, as we, brief incidents in the story of life, are accustomed to think of yesterday. It comprehends the whole three thousand million years of Organic Evolution. All through we have the same spectacle of beings over-running their means of subsistence and thrusting their fellows out of the normal way of life into strange habitats they would never have tolerated but for that urge to live, anyhow and at any price, rather than die.

For long periods, in our time-space system, a sort of balance of life between various species has existed, and their needless mutations have been eliminated. In the case, however, of a conspicuous number of dominating species and genera, their hypertrophy has led not only to an excess of growth over nutriment, but also in the case of those less archaic forms with which we are more familiar to a loss of adaptability through the relative importance of bigness over variation. The more they dominated the more they kept on being the same thing.

The continual fluctuations of normal Being in time, and its incessant mutations, confronted each of these precarious hypertrophied unstable dominating groups with the alternative of either adaptive extension of their range or else replacement by groups and species better fitted to the changing face of existence. Astronomical and internal planetary shrinkages in this universe of ours (which are all a part of the Time process) have, for example, produced recurrent phases of world-wide wet mud and given away again to the withdrawal of great volumes of water from a desiccated world of tundras and steppes, through the extension of glaciation. The sun is a variable star, but we can fix no exact term to its variations. The precession of the equinoxes is a wabble in the sequence of our seasons.

The same increasing discordance with the universe which we regard as real being, grows more and more manifest. Adapt or perish has been the inexorable law of life through all these ever intensifying fluctuations, and it becomes more and more derisive as the divergence widens between what our fathers were wont to call the Order of Nature and this new harsh implacable hostility to our universe, our all.

Our universe is the utmost compass of our minds. It is a closed system that returns into itself. It is a closed space-time continuum which ends with the same urge to exist with which it began, now that the unknown power that evoked it has at last turned against it. "Power", the writer has written, because it is difficult to express this unknowable that has, so to speak, set its face against us. But we cannot deny this menace of the darkness.

"Power" is unsatisfactory. We need to express something entirely outside our "universe", and "Power" suggests something *within* that universe and *fight* against us. The present writer has experimented with a number of words and phrases and rejected each in turn. "x" is attractive until one reflects that his implies an equation capable of solution in terms of finite being. "Cosmic process", "the Beyond", "the Unknown", "the Unknowable", all carry unsounded implications. "The Antagonism" by itself over-stresses the idea of positive enmity. But if we fall back on the structure of the Greek tragic drama and think of life as the Protagonist trailing with it the presence of an indifferent chorus and the possibility of fluctuations in its role, we get something to meet our need. "The Antagonist", then, in that qualified sense, is the term the present writer will employ to express the unknown implacable which has endured life for so long by our reckoning and has now turned against it so implacably to wipe it out.

As our minds have probed more and more curiously into the space-time continuum in which the drama of evolution has been framed, they have discovered one paradoxical aspect after another behind the plausible face of "normal" Being. The uranium-lead riddle, to which we shall recur, is only among the latest of these absurd posers.

For example we have realized quite recently there is a limit set to velocity. The highest speed at which anything can move is the velocity of light. It is an ingenious suggestion to compare our normal world to a three-dimensional system falling along a fourth dimension at that speed. But this fourth dimension through which it falls implies a residuum of the space-time continuum in which our "universe" is framed. All that space-time continuum is our "universe". It leaves us still with its evolutionary process and all the rest of it within the confines of our system.

The searching skepticism of the writer's philosophical analysis has established this Antagonist as invincible reality for him, but all over the earth and from dates immemorial, introspective minds, minds of the quality of the brooding Shakespeare, have conceived a disgust of the stress, vexations and petty indignities of life and taken refuge from its apprehension of a conclusive end to things, in mystical withdrawal. On the whole mankind has shown itself tolerant, sympathetic and respectful to such retreats. That is the peculiar human element in this matter; the recurrent refusal to be satisfied with the normal real world. The question "Is this all?" has troubled countless unsatisfied minds throughout the ages, and, at the end of our tether, as it seems, here it is, still baffling but persistent.

To such discomfited minds the world of our everyday reality is no more than a more or less entertaining or distressful story thrown upon a cinema screen. The story holds together; it moves them greatly and yet they feel it is faked. The vast majority of the beholders accept all the conventions of the story, are completely part of the story, and live and suffer and rejoice and die in it and with it. But the skeptical mind says stoutly, "This is delusion".

"Golden lads and lasses must, like chimney sweepers, come to dust."

"No," says this ingrained streak of protest: "there is still something beyond the dust."

But is there?

There is no reason for saying there is. That skeptical mind may have overrated the thoroughness of its skepticism. As we are now discovering, there was still scope for doubting.

The severer our thinking, the plainer it is that the dust-carts of Time trundle that dust off to the incinerator and there make an end to it.

Hitherto, recurrence has seemed a primary law of life. Night has followed day and day night. But in this strange new phase of existence into which our universe is passing, it becomes evident that events no longer recur. They go on and on to an impenetrable mystery, into a voiceless limitless darkness, against which this obstinate urgency of our dissatisfied minds may struggle, but will struggle only until it is altogether overcome.

Our world of self-delusion will admit none of that. It will perish amidst its evasions and fatuities. It is like a convoy lost in darkness on an unknown rocky coast, with quarrelling pirates in the chartroom and savages clambering up the sides of the ships to plunder and do evil as the whim may take them. That is the rough outline of the more and more jumbled movie on the screen before us. Mind near exhaustion still makes its final futile movement towards that "way out or round or through the impasse".

That is the utmost now that mind can do. And this, its last expiring thrust, is to demonstrate that the door closes upon us for evermore.

There is no way out or round or through.

II
MIND IS RETROSPECTIVE TO THE END

THE WRITER HAS already made the distinction between his very intermittent and specialized phases as a philosophical enquirer and the normal interests of his life. There he is just another ant, albeit sustained in his stoical acceptance by a rare and peculiar vision. But the masses of our fellow-creatures have not that vision to sustain them, and we have to square our everyday conduct to theirs.

There are large ambiguous masses of the formicary, whose leaders, unable to grasp what is happening, are resorting to the most evil and malignant magic propitiations to avert the distressful fate that closes in upon us all. Denunciation, which implements old prejudices with a new cruelty, flourishes. The unfortunate ant involved in these milling masses does his best to keep his faith to those to whom he has given himself over. So he may get away with it to the end. He may feel uncomfortable and disconcerted at times, but he and his associates will for the most part sustain an atmosphere of valiant futility, assuring themselves and one another that presently the old game will be resumed with all its present stress gone like a dream. And even before he is sufficiently awake to tell his dream of his world restored, he will have forgotten it and passed into nothingness for ever.

III
THERE IS NO
"PATTERN OF THINGS TO COME"

O UR UNIVERSE IS not merely bankrupt; there remains no dividend at all; it has not simply liquidated; it is going clean out of existence, leaving not a wrack behind. The attempt to trace a pattern of any sort is absolutely futile.

This is acceptable to the philosophical mind when it is at its most philosophical, but for those who lack that steadying mental backbone, the vistas such ideas open are so uncongenial and so alarming, that they can do nothing but hate, repudiate, scoff at and persecute those who express them, and betake themselves to the comfort and control of such refuges of faith and reassurance as the subservient fear-haunted mind has contrived for itself and others throughout the ages.

Our doomed formicary is helpless as the implacable Antagonist kicks or tramples our world to pieces. Endure it or evade it; the end will be the same, but the evasion systems involve unhelpfulness at the least and in most cases blind obedience to egotistical leaders, fanatical persecutions, panics, hysterical violence and cruelty.

After all the present writer has no compelling argument to convince the reader that he should not be cruel or mean or cowardly. Such things are also in his own make-up in a large measure, but none the less he hates and fights against them with all his strength. He would rather our species ended its story in dignity, kindliness and generosity, and not like drunken cowards in a daze or poisoned rats in a sack. But this is a matter of individual predilection for everyone to decide for himself.

IV
RECENT REALISATIONS
OF THE NATURE OF LIFE

A SERIES OF EVENTS has forced upon the intelligent observer the realization that the human story has already come to an end and that *Homo sapiens*, as he has been pleased to call himself, is in his present form played out. The stars in their courses have turned against him and he has to give place to some other animal better adapted to face the fate that closes in more and more swiftly on mankind.

That new animal may be an entirely alien strain, or it may arise as a new modification of the hominidæ, and even as a direct continuation of the human phylum, but it will certainly not be human. There is no way out for Man but steeply up or steeply down. Adapt or perish, now as ever, is Nature's inexorable imperative.

To many of us this crude alternative of up or down is intensely unpalatable. The forces that evolved us in the long succession of living beings endowed us with a tenacity of self-assertion that rebels against the bare idea of giving place to rats or unclean intrusive monsters equipped with streptococci for our undoing. We want to be in at the death of Man and to have a voice in his final replacement by the next Lord of Creation, even if, Oedipus-like, that successor's first act be parricide.

All over this planet are scattered the traces and achievements of Man, and it demands an intense intellectual effort from most of us to realize that this wide distribution of human products, is a matter of the past hundred thousand years. Radioactive substances and the process of radio disintegration must have begun in the solar system in a period of about three thousand million years and had already ceased long before life had become possible upon earth. Says Dr. N. H. Feather of the Cavendish Laboratory, Cambridge, in CHEMICAL PRODUCTS, Vol. 7, No. 11-12, Sept.-Oct. 1944:

"All radioactive species are 'natural' in the sense that conditions must have obtained at some stage in cosmic evolution, and probably still obtain in the interiors of the hotter stars, in which their production has taken place—and is still possible, but those conditions have not obtained on the earth since the time of its separation from the sun, and, as inhabitants of the earth, we conventionally regard as 'natural' only those radio elements which are found on our planet to have survived the period of some three thousand million years (3 x 109 years) since separation occurred."

Thereafter by degrees the planet became a possible habitat for this strange intruder, life. It span about the sun at what rate we do not know, nor at what distance, it acquired a satellite moon whose rotation was slowed down by a tidal wave until it turned its face towards its mother earth for ever. So a lunar month is a lunar day. Our own planet must be undergoing a similar retardation towards the sun, so that early years and ages of life on earth rushed by at a pace out of all proportion to these last deliberate ages. The machine was running with feebler brakes. Some- when in that headlong phase, under shelter of a dense cloud canopy of steam, the series of rhythms we call life, began.

In the invariable darkness of the deep sea, in the implacable dryness of the dry land, there were no rhythmic possibilities. It was, as Professor J. B. S. Haldane, in one of his admirable popular articles, has pointed out, in the intertidal belt only that they were to be found. Light followed darkness and darkness light, and life, that peculiar throb in matter, en- sued. The palaeontologist finds intimations in the record of rocks, of a lifeless phase of unknown duration, before the sunlight actually pierced the steamy veil and inaugurated the process called life.

The sequences of these opening rhythms are still indeterminate. They were elemental, so that their nearest analogies are to be found in the microscopic tissue elements of contemporary life or in the surface waters of the sea. There was a huge proliferation of diatoms and the like, and very early in the story some favourable mutation produced a green sub- stance, chlorophyll, which, in the presence of sunlight, produced a quasi- permanent, infectious compound so long as the light endured. So that the record of the rocks breaks abruptly from lifelessness into a variety of intertidal forms.

These forms in all their variety manifest one disposition in common, an élan vital, a drive to assert their being. They display in its crude begin- nings that "struggle for existence" which has become the fundamental theme of the history of life. Quite early this living stuff breaks up into individual fragments, which can meet varying occasions and survive here even if others dry up or otherwise perish there. These primitive individu- als seem free from any impulse of conflict either against the food they ingest or against one another. If they meet they will flow together and break up again apparently invigorated by the encounter. This rejuvenescence occurs without any sexual differentiation. It is an affair between equals.

But the establishment of a difference among individuals so that one set is specialized for adventure, experiment and ultimate death while another sort continued the species without ending, began very early in the history of life. The great majority of the many-celled beings upon this planet begin and end as fertilized ova. Some bud and break up; some are propagated by cuttings, by parthenogenesis (as with green fly) or the like, but such methods of reproduction keep the species fixed, inadaptable and vulnerable, and sooner or later, if there is to be survival, there must be a return for invigoration and variation to the male and female roles already established in their present form in the earliest chapters of the palaeontological record.

There are wide fluctuations in the differentiation of the sexes even in the same species, according to the changing imperatives of life. Few of us stay to consider the sex of a tiger or tigeress when we encounter it at large, but the sex of a passing cat or of a rabbit or hedgehog, or of a wolf in a pursuing pack or a fly or a lizard, is by no means obvious.

Even the stigmata of sex in *Homo sapiens* are far less conspicuous to-day than they were a hundred years ago. The exaggeration of the waist by tight-lacing has ceased. So also has much mysterious cosseting of girls. The bicycle played a part in that release. The growing girl braced herself up and went for a gentle ride on the new toy when her grandmother would have been resting in bed, and found herself better for it. At any crisis our great-grandmothers would "swoon", but who ever hears of women swooning to-day? Now men faint more frequently than women.

In a brief period, within the lifetime of an elderly man, the relations of the sexes in the British community, the age relations in marriage, the social readjustments consequent upon these changes, have been greatly changed. Older men used to marry and use up young wives; now the world is full of young couples and it is exceptional to meet wintry January married to blooming May. The pendulum may swing back. Or it may not be a pendulum swing we are contemplating. Deliberately planned legislation, food shortages and such like economic processes, waves of sentiment for or against maternity, patriotic feeling or the want of it, the natural disposition to fall in love coupled with a desire to fix a relationship by some permanent common interest, and a pride in physically and mentally well-begotten children, may play incalculable parts in the production of a new humanity, capable of an adaptation to the whirling imperatives about us, sufficient to see out the story of life on earth to its end.

It is claimed by various religious bodies that they protect "the institution of the family". They do nothing of the sort. The family has existed since animals bred and mated and went apart to protect and rear their young. But priestly intervention has degraded this clean and simple relationship by damning unborn children with the idea that they were "conceived in sin", making illegitimacy mysteriously shameful, and keeping all the fundamental facts and possibilities of family life from young people until it is too late for them to benefit by their knowledge.

V
RACE SUICIDE BY GIGANTISM

THE HUMAN INDIVIDUAL lives to a very great age, measured by the lives of the creatures about him. The Radium Clock gives us a maximum period of far less than ten and probably far less than five thousand million terrestrial years for the career of life. During all this period there has been a constant succession of forms, dominating the scene. Each has dominated, and each in its turn has been thrust aside and superseded by some form better adapted to the changing circumstances of life. Each has obeyed certain inescapable laws that seemed to be in the very nature of things.

First of these laws was the imperative to aggression. The fiat was live, and live as abundantly as possible. Live more than your brothers, grow larger, devour more. In the earlier days the imperative was unqualified by any impulse to mutual aid against a common competitor. So the big individuals ate up the food of the small ones, even if they did not actually eat them, and grew larger and larger. In the record of the rocks it is always the gigantic individuals who appear at the end of each chapter.

The planet spins, climate changes, so that the old overgrown Lord of Creation is no longer in harmony with his surroundings. Go he must. Usually but now always, some entirely different form of life succeeds him. Or like the sharks he may dwindle in numbers until the food supply overtakes him, and then, if nature has contrived no alternative in the meanwhile, he may return to his former abundance. Sharks and their kind live and die violently and nothing is left of them to fossilise. We know of huge contemporary basking sharks and the like. They may have grown to their present bigness quite recently or they may have basked for ages—as soon as there were sufficient fishes to be devoured. We are left guessing.

VI
PRECOCIOUS MATURITY,
A METHOD OF SURVIVAL

NATURE IN HER insensate play with the possibilities of life has produced some abrupt novelties in the record by accelerating the fertilization and ripening of the ovum relatively to the other phases of the life cycle. We must bear in mind always in these questions that it is a complete life cycle we inherit and not some fixed adult form. And time and after time Nature has cut out an adult form from the record altogether, abolished it, and made some larval stage the sexually mature form.

At one early phase in the record, the Echinoderms, the starfish and so forth, with their radiant structure, were Lords of Creation. They had little or no powers of locomotion in their adult state, and many, like the crinoids, were rooted to the rocks. Among other radiant forms the Tunicata had reverted to the production of cellulose and were markedly vegetative in their habit of life. They discharged their fertilized eggs into the water and dissemination of these was greatly assisted by the development of accessory structures that stiffened the drifting larvae and gave an independent impetus to their movement. The backbone of these traveling emissions has been christened the notochord, and the new fore and aft forms of life of which it was the precursor, are called the Chordata, as opposed to the series of forms without notochords, the Starfish, Sea Urchins, Sea Cucumbers and so on, which had hitherto been Lords of Creation. The whole vast world of backboned animals, including ourselves, owes its existence to this freak of nature. There was no reason whatever in it. It happened so.

The notochord appears in the development of all vertebrated animals, but in all the higher forms it is invaded and superseded by cartilaginous or bony matter. It persists through life in the hag-fish and lampreys, and in the lamprey it comes to our tables.

VII

The Antagonism of Age and Youth

THE WRITER ACCEPTS these facts of nature with tranquillity and would not have them otherwise. But he does not believe that any young man, younger than thirty-five, let us say, as a maximum, will accept them in the same spirit. Until round and about that age every younger man is in conflict with the universe and seeks to have his will of it. He must be a very under-vitalised being indeed to be ready to give in and "take things as they are".

But the present writer is in his seventy-ninth year; he has lived cheerfully and abundantly. Like Landor he has warmed both hands at the fire of life and now as it sinks towards a meticulous invalidism, he is ready to depart. He awaits his end, watching mankind, still keen to find a helpful use for his accumulations of experience in this time of mental confusion, but without that headlong stress to come to conclusions with life, which is a necessary part of the make-up of any normal youngster, male or female.

Every man over the formative years is in the same case as the writer. He made himself then. Since then he and all those other elder men have simply been working out and elaborating, with, in most cases, a certain ebb of intensity, the forms of thought into which they shaped their conviction. He is inclined to think that his continuing interest in biological science may have kept him in closer touch with living realities than is the case with politicians or money speculators or divines or busy business men, but that does nothing to bridge the gulf between an older man and the young. Hopefully or maliciously, jealously or generously, we old boys look on and cannot be anything better than lookers-on. We lived essentially, forty years odd ago. The young are *life*, and there is no hope but in them.

VIII
NEW LIGHT ON THE
RECORD OF THE ROCKS

THE ROTATION OF the earth and its annual circulation in its or-
bit is slowing down. All that has come to light in recent years
stresses this idea that, measured by the precisions of the Radium
Clock, our estimate of the duration of the early ages of the record of the
rocks must undergo a quite immense reduction relative to the Cainozoic
Period. The shapes remain the same but the proportions are different.
That secular slowing down may or may not have been continuous. That it
was seems the more probable thing to the writer. We do not know. The
conditions of individual and specific survival seem to have fluctuated very
rapidly and widely in those headlong times.

One thing is certain. Not one fact has ever emerged, in a stupendous
accumulation of facts, to throw a shadow of doubt upon what is still
called the "Theory" of organic evolution. In spite of the vehement deni-
als of the pious, no rational mind can question the invincible nature of
the evolutionary case. There is an admirable little book by A. M. Davies,
EVOLUTION AND ITS MODERN CRITICS, in which this case is fully and convincingly summarized. To that the ill-informed reader should go.

What does appear now, is this fact of the slowing down of terrestrial
vitality. The year, the days, grow longer; the human mind is active still
but it pursues and contrives endings and death.

The writer sees the world as a jaded world devoid of recuperative power. In the past he has liked to think that Man could pull out of his en-
tanglements and start a new creative phase of human living. In the face of
our universal inadequacy, the optimism has given place to a stoical cyni-
cism. The old men behave for the most part meanly and disgustingly, and
the young are spasmodic, foolish, and all too easily misled. Man must
go steeply up or down and the odds seem to be all in favour of his going
down and out. If he goes up, then so great is the adaptation demanded
of him that he must cease to be a man. Ordinary man is at the end of his
tether. Only a small, highly adaptable minority of the species can possibly

survive. The rest will not trouble about it, finding such opiates and consolations as they have a mind for. Let us then conclude this speculation about the final phase in the history of life, by surveying the modifications of the human type that are in progress to-day.

The Primates appeared as forest creatures related to groups of the Insectivora. They commenced arboreal. They acquired quickness of eye and muscular adjustment among the branches. They were sociable and flourished wider. Then, as the usual increase in size, weight and strength occurred, they descended perforce to ground level, big enough now to outface, fight and outwit the larger carnivores of the forest world. Their semi-erect attitude enabled them to rear up and beat at their antagonists with sticks and stones, an unheard-of enhancement of tooth and claw. But presently their sociability diminished because they now needed wide areas of food supply. The little fellows faded out before the big fellows, according to the time-honoured pattern of life. The great apes developed the institution of the private family to a high level. Along this line they traveled to the gorilla, the chimpanzee, the orang-utan of to-day.

But outside forest regions during a phase of forest recession, the developing primates were exposed to other exactions. Grass plains and arid steppes spread out. The supply of vegetable food shrank. Small game and meat generally became an increasingly important part of the dietary. As ever there was the alternative: "Adapt or perish". From a world-wide massacre of resistant primates a new series of forms had the good fortune to escape. They were more erect than the forest apes; they ran and hunted and they were sufficiently intelligent to co-operate in their hunting.

These cursive ground apes were the Hominidæ, a hungry and ferocious animal series. Since they are open air animals with sufficient wits to avoid frequent drowning, the fossil traces of their appearance are few and far between. But they suffice. If they did not leave many bones, they littered the world with implements. The erect attitude had liberated hand and eye for a more accurate co-operation. These brutes communicated by uncouth sounds. They seized upon stakes and stones for their purposes. They hammered great stones into a sharper shape, and when the sparks flew into the dry leaves amidst which they squatted and the red flower of fire appeared, it appeared in a manner so mild and familiar to them that they were not dismayed. No other living creature hitherto had seen fire except in a catastrophic stampede of terrified animals. It pursued relentlessly. Bears, even cave bears, bolted headlong from fire and smoke. The Hominidæ on the contrary made a friend and a servant of fire. Attacked by cold or carnivorous enemies, they countered by creeping into caverns and suchlike sheltered places and keeping the home fires burning.

So in the wintry phases of the successive glacial periods, these great quasi-human lout-beasts prevailed. With uncouth cries and gestures they hunted and killed. They were, in their adult form, much bigger and heavier than men. The clumsy hands that battered out the Chellean implements were bigger than any human hand. Skilled knappers can forge the relatively delicate implements of the later palaeolithic men with the utmost success, but the sham Chellean implement is as difficult as a subhuman eolith. The Chellean implement is the core of a great flint; the later human implement is a flake struck off from a core.

The creature called *Homo sapiens* emerges from among the earlier Hominidæ very evidently, as another of those relapses of the life-cycle towards an infantile and biologically more flexible form, which have played so important a role in the chequered history of living things. He is not the equivalent of the clumsy adult Heidelberg or Neanderthal man. He is, in his opening phase, the experimental, playful, teachable, precocious child, still amenable to social subordination when already sexually adult. The ever changing conditions of life had less and less tolerance for a final gross overbearing adult phase, and it was cut out of the cycle. That primordial gross adult *Homo* disappears, and gives place to a more juvenile type, that much the record shows very plainly, but the phases and manner of the transition remain still open to speculation. All varieties of *Homo sapiens* interbreed, and there may have been a continuous interbreeding among the earlier species of the genus. Intervals of isolation may have produced Neanderthaloid, negroid, fair, dark, tall and short local variations still able to interbreed—in the same way that the dogs have produced endless races that can and will mongrelize when barriers break down. Families and tribes may have warred against each other and the victors have obliterated their distinctiveness by mating with captive women. Comparative anthropology slowly disentangles this story of the way in which the now unnecessary primordial adult *Homo,* for all effective purposes, faded out, leaving as his successor the childlike *Homo sapiens,* who is, at his best, curious, teachable and experimental from the cradle to the grave.

These words "at his best" are the gist of this section. It is possible that there are wide variations in the mental adaptability of contemporary mankind. It is possible that the mass of contemporary mankind may not be as readily accessible to fresh ideas as the younger, more childish minds of earlier generations, and it is also possible that hard imaginative thinking has not increased so as to keep pace with the expansion and complication of human societies and organizations. That is the darkest shadow upon the hopes of mankind.

But my own temperament makes it unavoidable for me to doubt, as I have said, that there will not be that small minority which will succeed in seeing life out to its inevitable end.

২ ২ ২

ABOUT THE CONTRIBUTORS

RUDY RUCKER grew up in Louisville, Kentucky. Memorable volumes in his youthful readings were SEVEN SCIENCE FICTION NOVELS OF H.G. WELLS and Colin Wilson's THE OUTSIDER, the two books setting him on his path to be a long-winded beatnik SF writer. Rucker has published twenty-nine books, primarily science-fiction and popular science. An early cyberpunk, he also writes SF in a realistic style that he characterizes as transreal. His most recent nonfiction book was about the meaning of computation: THE LIFEBOX, THE SEASHELL, AND THE SOUL. His latest novel is MATHEMATICIANS IN LOVE, which gratifyingly includes the ouster of a corrupt and evil U. S. President. His latest story collection is MAD PROFESSOR. Having finally retired from his day-job as math and computer science professor, Rucker spends an inordinate amount of time writing and photographing for his blog www.rudyrucker.com/blog.

COLIN WILSON has written over 100 books. At 24, he was hailed as a major existentialist thinker when his first success, THE OUTSIDER (1956) was published. But in his many books, Mr. Wilson has consistently revealed his contention that insight is achieved during moments of well-being, attained through effort and focus and that pessimism is what robs people of their vital energies. He lives on the Cornish coast in England.

෨෨   ෨෨   ෨෨

www.ingramcontent.com/pod-product-compliance
Lightning Source LLC
Jackson TN
JSHW080855211224
75817JS00002B/49